MW01643996

the trouble with being god

William F. Aicher

ISBN: 978-0-615-25996-3

www.beinggod.com

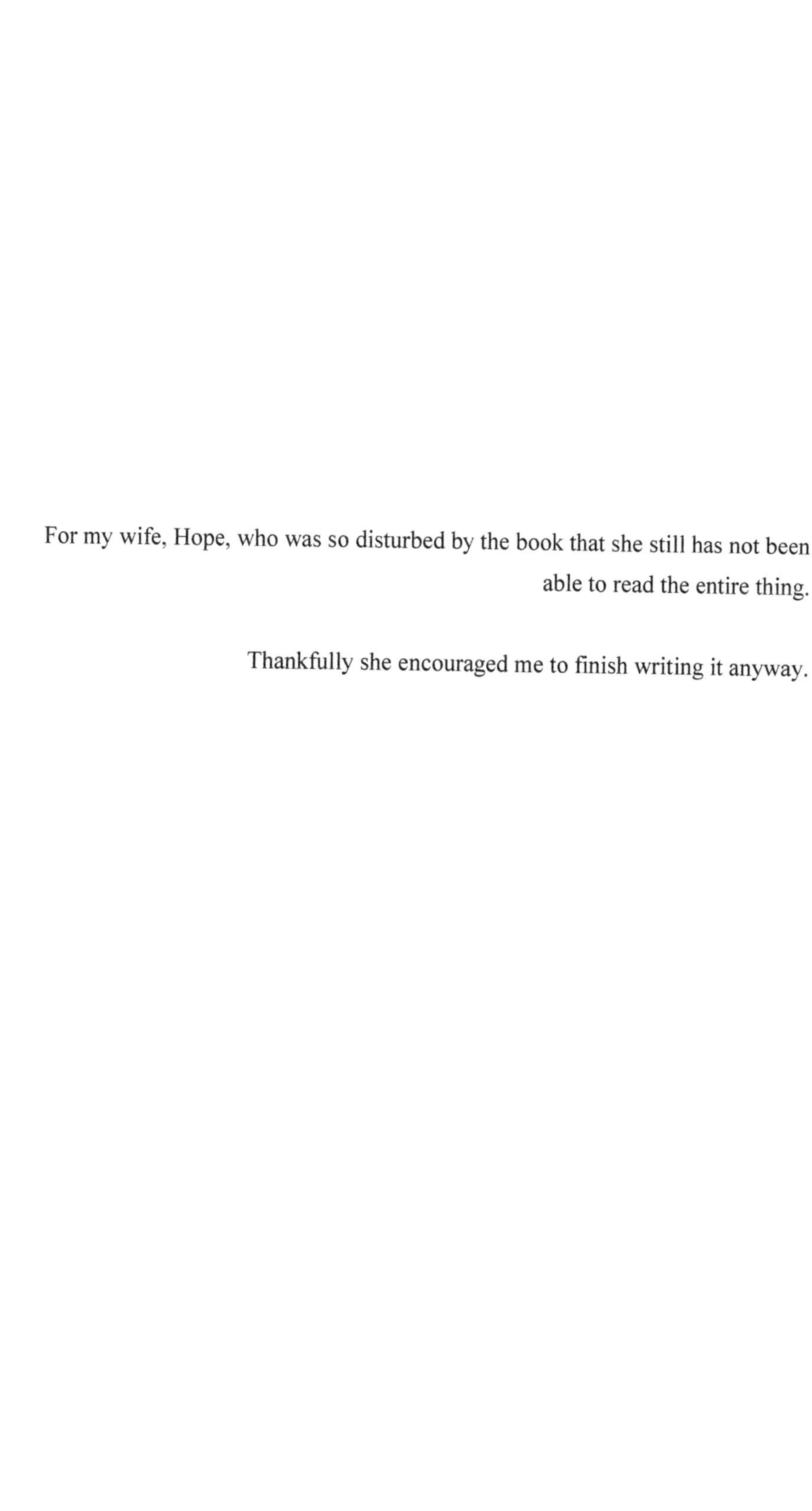

For my wife, Hope, who was so disturbed by the book that she still has not been able to read the entire thing.

Thankfully she encouraged me to finish writing it anyway.

Preface

Throughout my life, I have held a deep-seated love for music. It has always been a part of me, and a part of everything I do. My professional career has rotated around it, and it has been a source of joy, sadness, and solace.

It has always been my belief that music can tap deeper into our souls than simple words could ever hope to do. This is why the poets of yesterday have been replaced by the songwriters of today, and why certain songs will live on forever as true insights into our souls.

While writing this book, I was influenced by many things: people I met, events in my life, and most of all, music.

Therefore, music is an integral part of the telling of this story. Rather than being part of the story, I believe music can assist as another way to tell a story – to portray thoughts and emotions that are too delicate and precise to be described in words alone.

As you read 'The Trouble With Being God' you will come across a variety of footnotes marking preferred listening selections to go along with the mood or events of the book. Unlike the soundtrack to a movie, however, the best way to experience these songs and the passages that follow them is to listen to the music first, then read on.

Of course, enjoyment of 'The Trouble With Being God' is does not require listening to the music selections. They are instead provided as a supplement to the story, a kind of “director's cut,” if you will.

With this said, I urge you to read on and enjoy the story, listening with your ears and with your heart.

Day One

CIRCUMSTANCE[1]

[1]Play Audio: "Shuffle Your Feet" by Black Rebel Motorcycle Club (BRMC)

the trouble with being god

One

His hand brushed cross her neck, gently caressing her sweet pale skin. With a small razor nestled between his middle and ring fingers he began cutting. It was just a slight flesh wound, barely a scratch - just enough to draw a trickle of blood. Her eyes confessed her desire to scream, but the gun in his other hand, pressed firmly against her left temple, stifled this craving.

He ran his tongue along her neck. Once. Twice. The salt of her sweat thrilled his appetite.

Then, with a forceful stroke of the blade, the serious cutting began - his tongue following close behind to taste the weight of her blood. In short time, however, even this composure gave way to rancor and his impatient hand plunged the razor deep into her throat.

She tried again to scream, but was left with nothing but a gurgle. The blood gushed from the gash in her windpipe and he quickly moved aside to avoid being stained by the cascade. Missing him completely, it spilt over her naked body, down across her breasts, smacking wetly onto the bare concrete. As the outpouring subsided it gave way to a few throaty gurgles, until it was nothing but a pulsing trickle.

Her pleading eyes turned back in the head up toward the sky - up towards heaven and the god she so adored. But in the end it was he, the man with the blade, who controlled her fate.

He was in control. He was her god.

Two

Steven tossed the magazine across his living room onto the end table at the foot of his worn leather couch, knocking over a few photographs of Karen, his longtime girlfriend, in the process. He could clean it up in the morning – he was much too tired to care at this hour.

Karen had left her issue of *Cosmopolitan* at his apartment once again. And, once again, Steven found himself reading it. He tossed the magazine when he realized he had upgraded from simple perusing to actually reading. He had much better things to do at this hour, like go to sleep. The old brown couch sounded like a great idea; the bed was all the way in the next room.

It had been nearly an hour since Karen left the apartment after yet another argument, which at this point of their relationship was nothing out of the ordinary. Lately things hadn't been going as well as either of them really hoped for and this was just another in a string of arguments over something insignificant. Tonight's insignificance revolved around how much Karen had spent on her oil change and once again both sides had blown things out of proportion, leaving Karen no exit other than to storm out in a furor.

After resorting to the simplest solution, a half hour regimen of vodka and perusing *Cosmo*, his head was swimming. It was definitely time to go to sleep.

But then the phone rang. Unluckily for Steven the phone was within reach, lying right there on the coffee table. So, in spite of his better judgment, Steven answered.

"Hello?"

Three

Small puddles of water glimmered from a lone streetlight, like a diamond-painted sky in a little girl's dream. A collection of newspapers rustled slightly from the frosty lake breeze, instilling a serenity found only in the same girl's fairy tales. An unidentified body hung naked, crucified on the side of the old Stengler Brewery. The odor of death filled the brisk night air. A crown of barbed wire had been placed upon the decaying carcass's maligned head. It was 4:32 a.m. in South Courtsdale. It was a Tuesday.

People didn't talk much in this part of town, especially not to anyone who would have notified the authorities. The last thing these people wanted was a bunch of cops rooting around in their business. Besides, they knew the cops wouldn't care anyway. One more dead homeless man meant one less panhandler for them to deal with.

The air was cool for an October night, the temperature hovering in the low-forties. The thundershowers from earlier in the evening had subsided, but the air remained damp with a drizzly mist. Steven hadn't thought to bring along his jacket, but had instead thrown on his well-worn Notre Dame sweatshirt. The sweatshirt had seen better days, but it was his most comfortable; it had been his favorite since he bought it when he first moved to college.

The sweatshirt never left him cold, yet tonight he felt a biting chill run through his body. It was a chill harsher than the damp air. It was a chill that permeated his bones, coursing through him and leaving him frozen. He felt the chill when he looked into the vacant eye sockets of the desiccated corpse. Even though the eyes weren't there they were still looking at him - into him. The cold was unnatural; even had Steven been someplace else, as naked as this corpse on this cold October night, it would have felt warm in comparison.

"Steve! Over here!"

Steve. He had cycled through a lot of names or nicknames in his 29 years: Steve, Stevie, Esteban, Stevers; even Steve-O. Only Rick the kiss-butt intern at work called him Steve-O.

Still, a name doesn't make a person. Why should he care what someone calls him, he is still the same entity; the same living, breathing life force destined to endure existence until the day his number comes up. On that day a person's name definitely does not matter. On that final day the person is no longer a person, but instead is reduced once again to nothing more than carbon-based matter, returning to the earth from whence he came.

No, a name doesn't define a person – at least most of the time. Eugene was a different story though. Steven had met Eugene a few years back when he was just a simple beat reporter, fresh out of college. Steven had been assigned to cover Comic-Con, the annual comic book collector's conference in San Diego. Eugene was his choice for an interviewee. Steven has since improved his decision-making process.

Eugene was every bit as "Eugene" as the name sounds. It is a name that rings of horn-rimmed glasses, pocket protectors, and a full-on nasal vocal delivery. Eugene fit this description to a T; with a few added extras including pants with a waist past the navel, an atrocious salmon shirt (tucked in tightly of course), and pant cuffs at his calves. He broke every rule of fashion simultaneously, including wearing a belt and suspenders – *at the same time*. Yes, Eugene was as "Eugene" as they came.

In the time since then, Steven had come to the conclusion that a name may not make a person, but it definitely reflects on them. From this he decided no one was allowed to call him anything other than Steven. Parents, co-workers, friends – none of them called him anything but. Except of course for Miles.

"Hey Miles. What the fuck happened here?"

Although only just over six feet tall, Steven's closest friend seemed to dwarf him in comparison. Mostly this was due to the imposing form Miles put forth; the dark skin of his African-American heritage was stretched taught over the muscular body of an officer who spent much more time on the street than behind a desk. The light from the streetlamp above cast a shine like a halo from his shaved head.

"Not good bro. Definitely not good. Some vagrant stopped a cop car that was making its rounds out on the main strip. Jumped right in front of the god damn thing. Hall over there was driving. Scared the shit out of him; damn near pissed his pants."

Steven would have laughed, but he was still putting too much effort into keeping his nausea in check than to spend any extra energy on humor. Not that the body was *that* unnerving, but combined with the alcohol he had downed earlier, the rotting corpse was far from helpful.

"So even though the guy smelt of piss and liquor, Hall goes and checks out this "sign from God" the waif kept screaming about. When he finally got here and saw for himself, he puked all over and radioed in. I buzzed you as soon as I heard about it; figured it would be a cheerful story to grace the front page with. You know, right next to the story about that guy who ate the World's Largest Corn Dog the other day."

Steven ignored the joke. "So how long has the body been here? How was he killed? By hanging? Who is it? Shit man, I need more than a crucified body, some drunk hobo and a puking cop."

At this time the coroner arrived. The rest of the police force who had graced the area were still doing what cops do; dusting for fingerprints, collecting evidence, putting up "Police Line Do Not Cross" tape, and so on. Miles figured he should have been helping, but at least he was doing his part by keeping the press occupied. Of course the only press there was Steven, whom he had personally invited.

"Wanna get a closer look? Pick up some juicy details to wow your editor and horrify your fans?"

Steven nodded, but even this simple motion sent shots of pain through his head. What was he doing here at this hour? He should have been sleeping. He could have gotten the details he needed in the morning. There really was no need for him to be there right *now*.

As Miles escorted Steven closer to the scene, Steven could see a trinity of railroad spikes holding the body to the wall, one puncturing each hand and the third through the pair of joined feet, affixing the body to the wall. A rusty steel rod pierced the man's lower right abdomen. As the body was lowered and removed from the building, Steven noticed the rod pushed almost completely through the man's body. It stopped just short at his back, not quite puncturing the skin but causing a pronounced impression.

The man must have been dead or unconscious by the time his body had been erected for its showcase. Any responsive man would have fought against someone pounding spikes through his hands into the wooden boards of the brewery. Of course, there was also the possibility it could have been more than one person – one to hold the victim in place and one to hold the spike and swing the hammer. Or, maybe the victim was so terrified that he did exactly what he was told for fear of even more horrible consequences. Regardless, Steven felt sicker and more fascinated as each grisly scenario played out in his head, to a point where he almost felt envious of the amount of planning and care that had gone into the event.

In the absence of the body, a faint stain of the dead man's silhouette was the only reminder of what had been on display moments before. A greasy crucifix of death, it would remain for months until the rains washed it away. The police didn't have any intentions of cleaning it up.

"I guess I'll give you a call as soon as we have any clue as to what happened here or we issue an official statement."

Steven didn't even hear Miles. He was lost in his own world of questions. Who would do something like this? Who was this man who was forced to endure humiliation even in death? It was sick. This was all Steven was certain of. A grin washed over Steven's face. Yes, whoever did this was one sick fuck.

What a great story.

Four

Morning came with sunshine and bird song. It would have been a beautiful day if the night hadn't been filled with torturous dreams brought on by the images Steven hadn't been able to shake from his mind after leaving the scene. He dreamt of being stripped of his clothes. He dreamt of screams. He dreamt of pleads for life. He dreamt of pain.

Birds and sunshine offered no solace.

It was almost noon by the time Steven finally rolled out of bed. He had been writing for *The Courtsdale Courier* for just three years now, but they afforded him considerable freedom to pursue his own stories at his leisure. Quite possibly the best reporter this mid-sized city had ever seen, the paper was happy to cut him his weekly check provided he produce quality stories without too much time in-between. Writing was what kept Steven going; it was his drive – his reason to keep going on through to the next day, and each day brought something new in this line of work.

He had only recently begun writing crime stories. For the past few years his forte had been feature writing, with the occasional hard news story or exposé. Since he was a young child, however, he had harbored a fascination with the dark underbelly of society. Normal people tended to ignore the dark side of life, even though they all knew it was there. Steven was intrigued by it: by man's desire to pillage, rape, maim, and destroy his fellow man.

Yes, man's dark side fascinated Steven. It was a darkness that swelled within their hearts, yet rarely showed its face. But in those instances where man embraced his darkness and allowed civility to shed its smiling mask, Steven found a rare form of beauty - a sickening beauty of animalistic, savage tendencies – and what he believed possibly may truly lie in the hearts of men.

Rising from his bed, he heard a small crunch as his feet touched the floor. Whatever he was stepping on slid easily across the carpet; Steven grabbed the edge of the bed to regain his footing. He rubbed his hands up and down his face as he yawned, feeling the sharp bristle from two days of stubbly growth. Stretching his arms toward the ceiling, he took another step forward, this time feeling a squish. He lowered his eyes to the floor and was met by what was left of yesterday's pizza beneath his left foot, the day-old sauce and bell peppers grinding into the tan pile carpet. A Styrofoam plate creaked under his right foot; he must have knocked the slice off and onto the carpet as he got out of bed.

Steven's stomach growled. He hadn't been able to keep much down last night, especially after what he had seen out at the brewery. His new mission was clear: find some sort of sustenance – something to set his stomach at ease.

Upon searching the freezer, Steven came upon a two-pound package of ground beef. Completely covered in frost, it had been in there for a while. But it was frozen – it couldn't go bad frozen. Now this was a dilemma. The meat was frozen. How was he supposed to brown the meat when it was in brick form?

He took the beef into the bathroom and turned on the shower. If shower steam worked for straightening wrinkled shirts, it could do just as well as a defroster. After all, thought Steven, you can defrost chicken by running it under hot water – so why not beef? So Steven grabbed his two-pounds of ground beef, some clean clothes, and an ice-cold beer. His favorite cure for a hangover was to drink some more - and beer always tasted best in the shower.

Steven worked the shampoo into a rich lather. The smell of coconut extract was almost overpowering. Steven had run out of shampoo and was forced to use Karen's. So he smelt like a girl; so what? It didn't make him any less of a man. That's right. He was a man's man, what with his beer in one hand and package of ground beef at his feet. He was just about to rinse the soapy mess from his head when he heard the phone ring.

The phone call was probably important. No one really called him unless it was. Then again it could be the landlord calling again, demanding to know why he hadn't received the past two months' rent. Either way he knew he should answer. So, as he rinsed the shampoo from his hair with the one hand, he fumbled with the other blindly for a place to set his beer. He felt the bottle find the soap shelf, set the bottle down and heard it shatter as it slipped off the shelf onto the shower floor.

"Typical," he muttered as he jumped from the shower to grab the cordless phone off the floor.

"What."

"Hey Steve-O. How's it going?"

"Oh just fucking splendid. Fucking splendid. Is this important Miles?" Steven's mind was on his beer. Wasted - down the shower drain. Never to be enjoyed. It was a tragedy really.

"Actually yes it is. Remember the guy from last night? Oh yeah, of course you do. Why am I asking…? Anyway we got him down here at the morgue. Franklin is about ready to do an autopsy, and we thought we would invite you down for the festivities."

"Why are you doing an autopsy? I mean it's some homeless nobody. Someone probably just got bored."

"Did you *see* anything last night? Or were you too damn drunk to remember? The guy was *hung like fucking Jesus Christ* man. Obviously this is something we want to know about. Plus he wasn't even a homeless guy."

"What? Well then who is he?"

"I think you better just come down here. You ain't gonna believe this shit man."

Five

The air was stale and held a bitter taste. The concrete floors and empty halls echoed the clack of footsteps from Steven's scuffed brown loafers. A nun, in her black and white penguin's outfit, brushed past him, hurriedly moving in the opposite direction. Her head was bowed and she sobbed heavily as she passed Steven. Her body seemed to heave with each tear she produced. She didn't even appear to notice his presence.

Steven's love of religion was not a deep one. His Catholic upbringing was now a distant memory, a smattering of dust on his past. Although he attended catechism classes since kindergarten, and was even confirmed at age seventeen, he had long since ceased believing in God (or any higher power, for that matter) replacing religion with a strict materialism. Still, his knowledge of religion had not faded, and he was perplexed as to why a nun would be visiting a morgue, much less in full habit. *Must have come to offer her prayers up for a parishioner or something*, he thought.

As he continued down the hallway he paused momentarily, took a breath, and moved onward to the door. When he reached the door he stopped, this time for a bit longer - perhaps as long as a minute. Exhaling, he shook his head to bring himself back into the moment, the here and now. And he pushed the door open.

The air in the autopsy suite was stale, but not the same as the air in the hallway. Instead, this air tasted more sickening than bitter. Perhaps it was because Steven knew what went on in this room. Perhaps this difference was in his head. Perhaps, but probably not.

"Hey buddy! What do we have here?" Miles jumped slightly as the smack of Steven's shoes on the tile floor announced his entrance. He and Franklin, the coroner, were hunched over a table, looking at some papers and talking.

"Steve, get over here and take a look at this." Miles motioned toward the papers with a slight nod of his head.

"Oh boy you aren't going to believe what we have here," said Franklin. He was a mousy guy. Short – about 5'6" with light brown hair in a bowl cut and a pair of wire rimmed glasses. All he had to do was trade in his scrubs for a pair of black pants, white shirt, and black tie and he would be the perfect computer geek. No one would know he cut up dead bodies for a living. Instead he could tell the girls he was head of Information Technology for one of the upscale firms on the lower East Side; his pay was good enough that he could just about get away with it.

As Steven wandered over to the table, his eyes landed upon a sign on the far wall. "Hic locus est ubi mors gaudet succurrere vitae." It was Latin, however most of his college memories of Professor Gast's Latin 101 had long since faded through years of generous scotch applications.

"This is the place where death rejoices to teach those who live."

Steven's gaze quickly shifted to a perplexed stare into Franklin's eyes.

"This is the place where death-"

Steven cut him off. "I heard you the first time. Are you trying to creep me out? Because you know it won't work. I've seen this stuff plenty of times before." Steven's voice had taken on a sharp tone, not of petulance – but of uneasiness. It was true; he had seen autopsies and other such gruesome acts performed countless times, but he had never seen something quite like what he had seen last night. Franklin's muttered phrase had quickly taken Steven back to the night before; the empty eyes staring at him in his mind – staring *into* his mind.

"I saw you looking at my sign, and your eyes held a look of confusion, so I thought perhaps I should translate for you. That's what the sign means, 'This is the place…'"

"Where death rejoices… blah, blah, blah. Yeah. Like I said, I heard you the first time. Great sign - totally brightens the mood in here. I might have to get one for my apartment." Steven was beginning to get defensive, and the gloves had come off.

"It's more of a tradition really. A good luck charm if you will – the coroner's philosophy or motto. Most autopsy suites have them."

The simple conversation had become a game of hidden verbal attacks. The two had transcended gentle conversation and a level of hostility underwrote every word being spoken. Steven was easily annoyed by Franklin's matter-of-fact tone. He could tell Franklin was doing it to piss him off; and he was. What had begun as a simple glance had turned into a game almost as childish as "he started it."

"Steve, take a look at this." Thrusting piece of paper in front of Steven's face, Miles broke up their little game. "This is what I was talking about earlier on the phone. That wasn't just some homeless guy, it was-"

"Holy shit – Father Bergens…" Steven muttered as his eyes scanned the report Miles had given him. His eyes scanned further down the paper. "St. Mary's Church, Darlington. That's just out of town – about fifteen minute's drive from the South Side."

"That's right, buddy. When I got back to the precinct last night we ran a check on recent missing persons around the area. Father Bergens was the first to show up. He was first reported missing on Sunday when he didn't show up for the morning mass. Anyway, they sent forensics over to the church to lift some prints to compare to the ones we got from the body, and they matched up perfectly. In fact, you just missed Sister Katherine, from St. David's – you know, the big church in downtown. She stopped by to ID the body. Fucking scared the shit out of her I think. Her face turned as white as that sheet covering it up, once we pulled it back for the ID. Lady almost went into hysterics, crying and shit. But she did say it was him, and then we told her she better go. Sucked that she had to see it, but oh well – whatever gets the job done."

"Okay, enough with the chit-chat gentlemen. What do you say we cut this boy open? The coffee and banana I had for breakfast just aren't cutting it, and the sooner I get this out of the way the sooner I get to have some lunch."

Franklin motioned toward the autopsy table, a large slanted aluminum fixture about waist high. The edges of which were raised slightly so as to avoid spillage of blood and other bodily fluids onto the floor.

As they made their way to the table, Jeffrey, the diener, rose from the chair he had been occupying while reading the day's *Courier* waiting for the autopsy to begin. An African-American man in his early sixties, Jeffrey had been working for Courtsdale General for as long as Steven could remember. He was the only coroner's assistant the hospital had employed, at least since Steven had begun attending autopsies years ago. His tall stature had begun to diminish as time wore on, the years having taken their toll on the man. Withering features and wisps of gray in the tufts of his eyebrows only exaggerated this further. Still, he was in good shape for a man of his age, and he had no problem transferring the body from the cooler to the carriage then to the autopsy table. Little care was taken in the transfer, as Jeffrey had performed this task countless times prior and was full aware that little harm could be done to a lifeless body.

Throughout the transfer process not a word was spoken - Jeffrey rarely spoke. In the years Steven had known him (or rather been aware of him, seeing as how Steven knew as much about Jeffrey as he did any passing stranger in the street) he could only recall Jeffrey having spoken four, maybe five times; and only when spoken to first. These few instances, however, were easily recalled when thought about.

Each time Jeffrey spoke Steven was taken aback in slight shock by the strong, guttural voice held by this aging man. Far from feeble, it was the voice better fit to a young muscular man in the prime of his life. It was a train conductor's voice, the voice of a construction foreman – sure to bring any man (or machine) to attention. Perhaps it was the pairing of this steel-throated voice with a towering aged man that had in the past set Steven aback, or perhaps it was the odd mismatching of nature.

At any rate, the body had been placed on the autopsy table and Franklin was about ready to begin. The snap of latex on Franklin's hands as he donned his protective rubber gloves had also snapped Steven back into the room and he was now at full attention.

"Victim is a white male, 48 years in age. Name: Father Theodore James Bergens. Approximately 70 inches in height, body weighing in at 164 pounds. Eyes have been removed from victim's head by what appears to be a sharp tool, as evidenced by small cuts at edges of wound. Possibly small knife or razor blade."

"Notice the fixed lividity with a pooling of blood especially noticeable in his feet and hands." His eyes rose up toward Steven and Miles, who were standing across the table opposite him, then pointed with them back down towards the body where he held Father Bergen's limp right foot in his hand. "The bottoms of his feet are purplish blue; the same with the fingers. Distinguished lividity apparent in fingernail beds too."

Franklin pressed his right thumb against the right foot of the body. He held it for a few seconds then released, the foot causing a dull metallic thud as it hit the table. "Thumb pressure applied to feet lividity, no blanching apparent. Lividity is fixed."

The examination moved from the wounds on the feet to the similar wounds on the hands, wounds that had been caused from the railroad spikes that had been removed the night before as the body was removed from the wall. The memory was still far too fresh in Steven's mind, forcing him to take a deep swallow in order to continue on. "Clotted blood around puncture wounds indicates victim was alive when nailed to the wall, blood ran down the body and pooled in the feet post-mortem, further indication of man being alive when nailed to wall."

Franklin continued, "Scattered purple-black hemorrhages on lower legs of victim. Hemorrhages vary in length from one to three millimeters. Commonly found in victims of suicidal hanging with complete suspension."

"Secondary lividity slightly apparent on the back of body, especially in calf area. Probably due to repositioning of body post mortem, most likely after being removed from wall last night before being brought to autopsy. Minimal secondary lividity apparent. He obviously hadn't been on that wall for very long – certainly no more than twenty-four hours. I'll have a better estimate after I look more closely at the state of putrefecation and finish my internal examination. If you guys wanna head out of here, feel free. I doubt I will find much more important details with the internal exam – at least not until toxicology comes back and that will be a few days minimum."

Miles took a deep breath and sighed. "Well, I thank you for your time Franklin, even if we didn't really learn much more than that our assumptions were right. Let me know if you come up with anything new – otherwise just send the full report over when you get it done. Come on Steve, let's get going."

Steven didn't hear Miles as he was still looking at the body, wondering just what all happened that night. Was this just a coincidence? Why would someone purposefully choose Father Bergens? How many things in Bergens life, the life of the killer, and every other possible factor had to happen for him to be here looking at the Pastor of his girlfriend's church dead on a slab at this exact moment. What if Bergens would have had a bagel instead of a donut for breakfast? Would something as simple as that have changed his fate? Or was he destined to be in this very place at this very time… it made Steven wonder how much control he had over his own fate.

“Steven!” Miles punched him in the arm and Steven snapped back to reality again. “What is it with you lately man? You've been totally out of it. You on something’ or what?”

“Let’s get out of here, Miles. What do you say we get ourselves a drink - I sure as hell could use one.”

“Sounds good man. Definitely sounds good.”

Six

"Give it back! Give it back, David, I had it first! Give it back or I'm telling. Ow! Karen, David hit me! Kaaar-ennnnn!"

Karen took one last drag from her cigarette before extinguishing it, sighed, and went back inside. "Why do I put up with this?" she thought. "I can't even turn my back for a minute and something goes wrong. All I wanted was one lousy cigarette… God knows I need it."

Dakota sat upon the ground crying, David was nowhere to be seen. The rest of the kids at KinderKind daycare center were busy playing with the various toys that had been spread out all over the floor. Karen knew she shouldn't have left them alone, but last night was a long one and the kids weren't helping to calm her nerves any. She had been trying to quit smoking, more because of the bad example it set for the kids than the potentiality of health complications. The kids couldn't get into much trouble in the two minutes it took for a quick smoke. Then again, maybe they could.

She rushed over to Dakota. "Dakota… Dakota what happened?" Dakota Paluniak was the sweetest little four-year-old Karen had ever laid eyes on, and had been coming to KinderKind since he was a baby. The lone son of a single father, Dakota's mother had died during childbirth.

His father, John Paluniak had been bringing him to KinderKind weekdays while John himself worked at Liberty Mutual. Being a single parent was no simple task, but he trusted KinderKind, especially Karen, who had already established herself as both capable and compassionate years before he began bringing Dakota in. Karen had been a friend of Shawna, Dakota's mother, and John placed the same trust in Karen as he had placed in his wife.

"David hit me," Dakota managed to spurt out between bouts of streaming tears. Although a sweet boy, Dakota had little tolerance for pain and managed to exaggerate the extent of his discomfort on more than one occasion.

"David hit you, huh?" Every daycare Karen worked for in the past had its troublemaker, but KinderKind was different. For the most part the kids all got along, save for the occasional encounter. And usually when these happened, as bad as Karen felt for thinking it, the kid sort of had it coming. Still it was her duty to keep the peace and make sure all the kids were sent home at night unscathed. "Where did he hit you, Dakota?"

"Here." He lifted his right hand to point to his left shoulder. The crying had stopped, but his eyes were still bloodshot and wet with a few tears remaining on his cheeks. Karen pulled her right hand back into the sleeve of her sweatshirt and wiped the tears with her cuff.

"There, there Dakota. It's okay. You're a tough little man, I'm sure you'll pull through." She placed her hand on his right shoulder and offered a smile. "Isn't that right, tough guy?"

Dakota pulled back his shoulders, took a deep breath, pushed out his chest, and grinned. "Yep. I'm tougher'n I look! I'm alright."

"Thatta boy. Since you are fine I am going to go find David and give him a good talking to. Don't worry, I won't tell him you told me. I'll tell him I saw from the window – no worries."

As Karen rose from her kneeling position she noticed a white van in the parking lot through the large picture window. Her glance shifted to the main door where a young man in his early twenties stood. Donning a pair of well-worn jeans, a dark green T-shirt, and a tattered blue baseball cap, he held a small bouquet of flowers in one hand and a clipboard in another.

"Karen Davis? Are you Karen Davis? I got some flowers here for a Karen Davis."

Karen's eyes lit up as she made her way to the door, eyes set on the flowers in the delivery boy's arms, feet gracefully avoiding the toys scattered about the floor. She traversed this children's gauntlet - seemingly oblivious to the dangers a misplaced foot on a Tonka truck may pose to an unwary ankle.

"I'm Karen Davis," she quipped happily. "Are those for me?" Her cheeks, usually soft and pale, now flushed with a hint of rose as dimples formed at the corners of her mouth, birthed from a blushing smile.

The delivery boy took one short step back and cocked his head to the side, to get a better look at her. Starting with her small sandal-clad feet, his eyes slowly ventured up her slender legs. She was wearing a cream colored sundress with a light yellow sunflower pattern. Her brunette hair was cut in a bob, and bits of hair had fallen against her high cheekbones.

"Yeah – flowers for Karen Davis…" his voice trailed off. Lost in her deep gray eyes he was more interested in Karen than in the delivery of the flowers. "Just sign here." He lifted his clipboard, refusing to take his eyes off of her. “So, um, yeah. My name’s Zach. Listen, if you’re not doing anything later, do you maybe wanna-“

With a quick swipe of her hand she signed the boy’s form and picked the card from the bouquet she had been bestowed. “Oh my God, they’re from Steven!” She cut him off abruptly, paying no mind to the delivery boy’s come-ons. The boy grunted slightly, turned about, and left down the entrance hallway.

Karen,

I thought you might like these. I apologize for last night; I was being a jerk. Anyway, I hope your day is going better than mine. Love you sweets – talk to you soon.

-Steven

She beamed as she re-read the card. Things had been a bit rough lately, and it was true that last night hadn’t helped matters. Still, she knew he had been having trouble sleeping the last few days and she had been under considerable stress herself. Things would eventually work themselves out; it would just take some time. It was the little things he did, like sending her flowers at work that made all the problems seem to fade away into unimportance.

Karen took the flowers into the kitchen. Still lost in the moment, she quickly put them in water as soon as she heard Dakota’s crying recommence. “Shit,” she thought as she glanced at her watch. “Can’t that kid learn to stand up for himself? This is going to be a long day… still only a quarter of two.” She took a deep breath and grabbed a box of cookies – supple ammunition for the battle ahead.

Seven

A Bryan Adams song played from a small radio behind the counter. It wasn't very loud and the sound was tinny with treble from the small speakers, but it was enough to give Barry something to listen to as he worked the line. When it was busy you couldn't even hear the radio from the front of the diner, the voices of customers and the busy clatter of dishes and cheap silverware easily overpowering its tiny speakers. Steven couldn't remember the song's name, only that it was from that Robin Hood movie with Kevin Costner. He liked the movie, but hated the song – and for that reason he longed for the business at Barry's Diner to suddenly explode.

"What can I get you boys?" Debbie was their waitress, as was often the case. Steven and Miles frequented Barry's, enjoying its peaceful calm in the afternoon. Earlier in the day, during the lunch rush, the place was undoubtedly bustling with activity. Nestled in one of downtown's few quiet hideaways, the little shop managed to bring in big business from downtown office workers looking for a place to unwind while they escaped the daily grind of cubicle life.

Steven and Miles generally liked Debbie, her personal demeanor and friendly smile were always a welcome change to an otherwise hectic day.

Debbie generally liked them as well, they never bitched about the food and they always tipped her generously, unlike the lunch hour cubicle rats.

"I'll have the Philly combo - hold the tomatoes. Oh, and can you bring out a pitcher of water?" Steven had decided against getting a drink, instead opting for a bite to eat and some water to flush his system of his lingering hangover. He still hadn't gotten a chance to eat that day, and he frowned as he remembered his ground beef still on his shower floor. It had probably defrosted by now.

"Just the soup for me, Deb." Miles had eaten a late breakfast, and the thought of eating still didn't agree too well with his stomach after his visit to Franklin's sterile white dungeon earlier that day. Despite that fact that he had been working homicide for several years now and had seen a number of bodies, he still hadn't gotten used to them. He hoped he would never get used to them.

"Alright. And you just want water too, right Miles?"

Miles nodded his head and she walked back to the counter. The two looked on as she walked away, eyes intently focused on their target. She was an attractive woman, in her late twenties. Her ash brown hair, tied in a ponytail, hung down to that point where her neck met her back, as she had worn it that way since she started working at Barry's. An apron wrapped taught around her slim waist left just enough open space in the back to give onlookers a generous view of her posterior. She knew this of course, and wore her clothes as such for just that reason. It was nice to have men find her attractive; even ogle over her if it meant for a bigger tip.

"You know, I saw Debbie in the park the other day. Over at Friar Park – she was Rollerblading. Don't know how she can still go out and do that in this weather. Too damn crappy out for me," said Steven, his gaze still focused on the door to the back kitchen area where she had disappeared moments before.

"Oh yeah? She with her man?" Debbie had been dating some guy named Aaron something-or-other for a while now. He was her typical hunk – in his mid-thirties, well built, and more than likely than not, unemployed. Steven saw the two at the park on more than one occasion but never made an effort to start a conversation. Besides, most of the time she was more than what one would call "preoccupied" with Aaron, and it wasn't like Steven and Debbie were close friends. If anyone were friends with Debbie, it would have been Karen – the two of them managed to yammer to no end whenever Karen came into the diner with Steven. Yet a friendship was unlikely as Karen often complained about Debbie and her lifestyle choices once she and Steven would leave the restaurant. In fact, in one instance, she had even gone so far as to refer to Debbie as "that tramp."

"Nahh, she was alone I think. Although I did see her talking to a few different guys off and on – not that I was paying attention or anything. In fact, come to think of it, I haven't seen her with what's-his-name for a while now. Maybe they broke up or something."

"There you go – now's your chance to make a move Steve!" Miles joked as he reached across the table and jabbed at Steven's shoulder.

The conversation came to an abrupt halt as Debbie walked toward their table and dropped off a glass pitcher filled with ice water. She looked inquisitively at the two. Yet neither looked at her, both keeping their mouths shut until she rolled her eyes and left the table to wait on the only other customers in the diner – a couple seated three booths down.

"Would you knock it off already? I'm just trying to enjoy some nice peace and quiet and here you are being a bitch." Steven's dour demeanor had finally lifted, and the two were joking around as per usual. "You don't stop it, and we're going to have to take this outside."

"Yeah, yeah – calm down will you? I can't take you anywhere anymore. Christ – if you want me to get her number for you all you have to do is ask. Forget it – I'll ask her for you next time she comes over here."

"Fuck… off."

Miles let out a full-bodied laugh, his muscular stature heaving as he did so. "So, how was your day Steve? Having fun yet?" He had decided to drop the subject of Debbie and leave poor Steven alone, opting to change the subject to something a bit more serious.

"Definitely interesting, man. Wow, I mean that was pretty intense shit this morning. Fucked up is actually the best way to put it. And this weather isn't helping to cheer me up either." Steven's gaze shifted to the window next to their booth and Miles's eyes followed suit. It had started to rain again – not a downpour but instead another miserable mist. For the past week the weather had been remarkably dreary, drizzling off and on with the occasional thundershower. The thermometer hadn't broken the fifty-degree mark for six days – well below average for October in Courtsdale.

"Yeah I hear you on that one," sighed Miles. "Thalia has been hounding me lately to take the kids out somewhere." Thalia and Miles had lived together as man and wife for what was nearing eight years now. They had three children together, all boys. Desmond, who had recently begun second grade, was the oldest - born only three months after their marriage. The other two, Devin and Mark, were fraternal twins who bore little resemblance to one another. They had just enjoyed their fifth birthday party, a raucous bash ultimately involving more police than just their father. Miles was often amazed by just how much trouble his pair of kindergarteners was capable of.

"She says they're driving her insane since they have been inside all the time lately because of the weather. 'All they do is play videogames and they never clean up their mess,' she says. I think we're going to catch a movie this weekend. Not sure though. Say – how have you and Karen been? You haven't mentioned her yet today – not like you."

Steven looked toward the kitchen door, hoping to see Debbie coming toward them, meals in hand. He didn't have much desire to discuss his and Karen's current situation, and the delivery of lunch would work as an ample distraction. To his dismay, however, Debbie was nowhere to be seen. The couple three booths over had, in the meantime, paid for their meals and left the diner, leaving Steven and Miles as the only two customers. An uncomfortable silence fell upon the room, the only sound being the radio – which had long ago moved past Bryan Adams and was currently playing some song by Neil Young. Steven wasn't sure as to the name of the song, only recognizing it by the signature vocals.

His eyes shifted down to his glass which he was obsessively rubbing his fingers back and forth across, although he hadn't realized he was doing so. It was something he did when he was nervous. Seeing no distraction to allow for easy escape, Steven had no choice but to indulge Miles's question with an honest answer. "Well, to tell you the truth, things have been a little off and on with us lately, Miles. I mean, most of the time everything is going good – but we have been fighting a lot more than usual. I'm not sure what is up, but it isn't good – that's for certain. Like last night, we got into a fight over the stupidest thing. It's probably my fault though, even though I know I'll never admit it to her. I've just been on edge lately, I guess."

"You've got to watch that, Steve. She's a good girl – but I'm sure you know that. You have to -" At this moment Steven's cell phone rang, stopping Miles mid-sentence.

"Steven." He answered the phone, half annoyed at the disturbance, half grateful for the interruption.

"Steven, it's Fred," said the voice on the other end. "How are things?" Holding the phone to his ear with his right hand, he looked to Miles and held up the index finger of his left hand, telling Miles to hold on with the conversation. Fred was his editor and boss; he had to take the call.

"Oh, well, umm, things are good Fred. What's up?" Fred never called unless there was a pressing issue. Well, that or he needed some sort of favor from Steven. The last time he called it was to ask for a ride to the airport, not exactly the top of Steven's list of fun activities, but something he had to do nevertheless if he wanted ensure the security of freedom he had been afforded at his job.

"You read the paper this morning? Never mind, of course you did – it's part of your job." Steven had not read the paper and he smiled at Fred's assumption; Fred always assumed the best of Steven, and Steven was grateful for this because it allowed him to get away with much more than he should have been able to. "Well, I'm calling about that homicide out at Stengler Brewery last night. I originally gave the story to Simkin, but that was before I got the full police report this morning. Did you know that the guy was Father Bergens, from St. Mary's over in Darlington? You know as well as I do that there is no way in hell that Simkin can do justice to this story – I just figured it was some homeless guy and there wouldn't be another word about it. And for that reason I extend my congratulations to you, for the story is now yours. By the way, where are you? I haven't seen you around here in a while."

Steven heard the kitchen door open as he listened to Fred spout on about the story. Chances were he already knew more about the case than anything Fred could tell him, but he felt compelled to indulge Fred's feelings of importance nonetheless. Through the kitchen door came Debbie, their meals in hand. As she placed them upon the table she looked at Miles who mouthed "his editor" to her. She nodded to signify her understanding, then turned her head to Steven and offered a warm smile.

"Actually I'm already a step ahead of you Fred. I'm down at Barry's with Miles right now; we just came from Franklin's to see the autopsy. I was down at Stengler last night too, Miles called me down there. So don't worry – I was planning on doing a story on it anyway. It is interesting, to say the least."

"Yeah, I know you were down there last night. Simkin said he saw you there, and I just got off the phone with Franklin and he mentioned you were down by him today too. Oh, and I need the story for tomorrow morning's paper. I need a full feature-length story, long enough to fill the front page, by six o' clock tonight, at the latest. That will give me plenty of time to edit it and get it to press."

"Christ Fred, how the hell am I supposed to do that? That only gives me," Steven pointed to his wrist, looking to Miles for the time.

"Three and a half hours Steven," Fred interjected. "You've got three and a half hours to get it done and on my desk. I told you what I need; now you just make it happen." Steven heard a click and then silence as Fred hung up. His editor had spoken; to argue would be an exercise in futility.

He closed his phone and shifted to face Miles. "Hey, sorry but I have to go. Fred wants a story by six, and I'll be lucky to get it done as it is."

"Not a problem. Need me to send anything over?"

"Yeah, if you could fax me a copy of the official police report, as well as whatever Franklin found in his autopsy, that would be great."

"Well, I'll send over what I can get my hands on. Besides, I have to get back to the office now. Your information will probably be sent over before you even get home. Give me a call if you need anything else – you know where to find me."

Steven stood up, drank down what was left of his water, grabbed his sandwich and made his way for the door. It was true, he had planned on writing a story on this case, but he hadn't planned on writing it today. It was as if he was being treated like a beat reporter again, saddled with deadlines and demands from an unrelenting editor. His only satisfaction lie in the fact that he was bestowed the story because Fred believed in him. As he got into his car, a silver 1993 Honda Civic, only one thought was in his mind: 6:00 was going to come way too soon. And it was going to take him at least a half hour to get home.

"I don't need this," he muttered, as he turned the key and the car's little engine sputtered to life.

Eight

Father Theodore Bergens of St. Mary's Church, Darlington, was found dead early Tuesday morning.

"Alright, that sucks." He moved his finger to the backspace key, clearing the screen.

Tuesday morning's murder on the lower east side ended up being...

"That one is even worse than the others. Come on Steven, this shouldn't be this difficult. It's just a lead – this should be easy." After fifteen minutes sitting at his computer, Steven had yet to come up with an opening for the story. For the most part, leads came easily to him. They flowed from his fingers like honeyed words from the lips of a poet – for the most part. Today he couldn't get into his flow. He stared blankly at the screen, then at the stack of papers on his desk: the faxed police report, Franklin's preliminary findings, his Moleskine notebook where he had scrawled a few notes before returning to bed after last night's excursion.

Father Theodore Bergens, former priest of St. Mary's Church, Darlington, was found dead early Tuesday morning in what police had at first labeled a random homicide.

He smiled. “Ah yes, that’ll work - for now at least.” Glancing at the corner of his computer screen he noticed the clock had already passed the 4:30 mark. *This story is going to end up being complete crap*, he thought. *Oh well, I might as well get going.*

After working on the story for nearly an hour, he heard the sound of rattling keys outside the door. Before he had time to get up, however, Karen had burst through the door and dropped her purse to the floor. She scurried over to Steven.

“Oh Hun, thanks so much for the flowers!” Her mouth once again opened to that full, blushing smile Steven had come to adore and he smiled as she planted a thankful kiss upon his surprised lips.

“Hey, no problem sweets. I really am sorry about last night; I don’t know why I let stuff like that bother me.”

“Don’t worry about it Steven. I shouldn’t have gotten all bent out of shape either. Well anyway I have to hit the shower. Care to join me?” Her smile gave way to a grin, and she winked her eye slyly.

Steven felt his heart leap, then his stomach sink as he remembered his promise. “Well babes I’d love to, but I have to get this story done for Fred by 6:00. Think we can drop it off on the way to dinner? It’ll only take a minute.”

“Awww.” Karen forced a frown, pushing her bottom lip into a full pout. Her grey eyes widened to create the best puppy dog face she could muster. “You can take a quick break can’t you? I’m sure Fred’ll forgive you so long as you give him a few juicy details. I see how he looks at me when I come in to visit you at the office.” She winked again, performing the best temptress act she could gather at such short notice.

"Sorry Hun, but this one can't wait. It's a pretty big story and I *have* to get it to him or he is going to have my ass – which would basically rule out you getting any." Steven didn't have the heart to tell her just yet that he had, just a few short hours ago, been witness to the autopsy of the man who had given her spiritual counsel since her childhood. He especially didn't want to make mention of the consequences surrounding his death, something which he was sure to send her into what he called "feminine hysteria." He wanted Karen in good spirits tonight, and the news would surely put a damper on the evening. It was best he told her later, waiting a few hours wouldn't hurt.

"Fine, fine. I'm just going to have to have fun without you then." Flipping a towel over her left shoulder, she spun to face the door. She made sure to overemphasize the sway of her hips as she did so – one last attempt to lure him in. Steven made no move to follow; his eyes were already focused back on the computer screen. Karen saw this and stuck her tongue out at him before she walked into the bathroom.

"Steven, what the hell is this?" Karen roared. "Why is there meat in the shower? Damn – and broken glass?! You know what – forget it. I'll clean it up." She was more perturbed than upset, the mess was just another thing she was forced to deal with that she shouldn't have had to. Their relationship had been full of little things like this lately, yet most of the time she managed to ignore them.

After what seemed like an eternity, Karen emerged from the bathroom. She had transformed into an angel, a task that took little effort on her part as Steven always thought she looked like one (a bitchy angel at times yes, but an angel nonetheless). In the meantime he had finished writing the Bergens story, saved it to his flash drive and shut down the computer to avoid the possibility that Karen would read it and learn about the murder.

"Damn girl! Come here and gimme a kiss."

"Nope, you had your chance lover-boy, and you missed it." She let out a small giggle, and then added, "Oops, I forgot - you were too busy with your story."

Steven paid no mind to her sass and before she knew it he managed to steal a begrudged kiss.

"You dick! Did I say you could kiss me?" Karen giggled. "I don't think I did. Let me think back... nope, can't say I recall ever giving you permission."

Steven kissed her agin, this time on the forehead, before heading to the bathroom. He too needed a shower. As he shut the door Karen grabbed the remote and flopped onto the couch, only to be surprised by a loud yelp from below.

"Oh hey there Mr. Stinky! I didn't see you lying on the couch. Did Steven feed you yet today?"

Steven's buck-toothed tabby cat, Mr. Stinky (real name Banky) had inherited the name Mr. Stinky from Karen. She harbored a penchant for calling things by names reflecting that which they were not. Mr. Stinky, or Banky, actually did not stink at all – and in fact held a rather pleasant odor, unlike many cats Karen had gotten to know over the years. Not that air freshener companies were beating down Steven's door to fashion a new scent after him, but as far as cats went, Karen thought Mr. Stinky smelled quite nice.

"Rrrrow. Rrrow," replied Mr. Stinky. She had no literal translation for what Mr. Stinky had said, but luckily for him she knew Steven well enough.

"I bet he forgot all about you, didn't he? Well let's get you something to eat." Karen, who had remained standing after her realization the couch was already spoken for, made her way to the kitchen and retrieved Banky's bag of cat food from the cupboard. "Here you go freak, eat up." Unlike Steven, Karen did not care much for cats. It wasn't that she hated them, but it wasn't that she harbored an intense love for them either. The only reason she put up with Mr. Stinky was because he managed to stay out of her way. He let Karen to her business, and she let Mr. Stinky to his.

Several minutes after staking her claim on the couch, while Mr. Stinky inhaled his dish of food, Steven rushed out of the bathroom. Pantless, he flew through the living room, past Karen, and into the bedroom.

"Shit, shit, shit," he grumbled as he avoided the couch. "We've only got ten minutes to get down to the office. You ready to go Karen?"

No, you've only got ten minutes to get to the office. I have all night, was the first thought to enter her mind.

"Yeah, I've been ready for a while," she yelled in the direction of the bedroom, just loud enough to overpower the television. "Did you know you forgot to feed Mr. Stinky? Don't worry – I took care of it."

Steven emerged from the bedroom, now fully dressed. His hair remained a damp exploration of organized chaos, but after running his hand through it a few times he decided it was good enough. "Alright then, let's go." He grabbed the flash drive from the computer's USB port and the two headed out the door.

The offices of *The Courtsdale Courier* were a short drive from Steven's apartment. And, while it could still take up to an hour to make it there during rush hour, they made the trip in a little under ten minutes. Throughout the drive he managed to avoid the subject of work, the story, or anything that happened with him since Karen left his apartment the night before. Instead he opted to ask her about her day. He didn't particularly care, as pretty much every day at the daycare sounded the same as the last to him, but he knew Karen liked to talk and any way to avoid the whole Father Bergens subject was fine by him. Besides, it allowed him to play the part of the caring boyfriend – which was sure to score him points and hopefully lead to some make-up sex later that evening.

"Do you want to wait in the car while I run up? It should only take a minute." Steven desperately hoped she would stay in the car, and his dreams were fulfilled with her reply.

"Yeah I'll stay down here. I want to get to The Connection before it gets too late, and besides I don't feel like getting sucked into conversation with Fred again - so try to keep it quick, okay Steven?"

The French Connection (or The Connection, as it had been dubbed by the hipster crowd) was a little club in the heart of downtown. Known for its burgers by day, The Connection underwent a transformation by night, morphing into one of Courtsdale's more popular hangouts. The kitchen closed at eight o' clock, leaving them precious little time to grab a meal. Karen would undoubtedly want to stick around after dinner for a few cocktails, and given his penchant for their sidecars, Steven was likely to agree.

A fairly small paper, especially for a city of Courtsdale's size, *The Courier's* offices were far from extravagant. By the time Steven walked in most of the staff had left for the day. Those few writers who remained would soon be gone as well, once they put the last bit of polish on their stories before handing them in to their respective editors.

"The prodigal son returns! How's it going Steve-O? I figured you were passed out somewhere for the last week – haven't seen you around here in a while."

Steven ignored Simkin's prodding and headed through the newsroom to Fred's office opposite the main door.

Fred, a heavyset man in his late fifties, had worked for *The Courier* since his graduation from the community college over in Darlington many years prior. He had begun his career as an intern (gopher) for the office, but over the years he gradually worked his way up the ladder through a series of promotions. His first assignment was the police beat – scanning police reports and reporting on various fires and automobile accidents. Still, through his perseverance and keen attention to detail he snuck his way into editorial, and was now secure in the comfortable position of Local Editor.

As Steven entered the office Fred looked up from his desk, peering over a pair of brass wire rimmed glasses perched upon his fat nose. "Ah Steven, just the man I have been waiting for. Let me see what you have."

Steven handed Fred the flash drive with the story.

"I still don't understand what your problem is with e-mail, Steve."

Fred put it into the computer and loaded the file. He scrolled through the document to the end and said, "Sorry Steven, but I need more than this. Thankfully-"

"Don't tell me you had Simkin write the story and I ended up doing this for nothing. Don't tell me that Fred."

"That's not it. That's not it at all. I definitely need your story. In fact, I need it more now than before, what you have here is good. Your work is excellent as usual Steven, but... " He paused and inhaled deeply through cavernous nostrils, scratching the sandy red hair upon his head as he did so. "What I was saying was, thankfully … well, how should I put this?" He paused again to place his hands on his desk before speaking again. "Thankfully you're here. Congratulations Steven, your story is taking over the *entire* front page, but for that I am going to need you to stretch your word count a bit."

"What the hell, Fred? You told me lead story and that's what I wrote for you. I have Karen waiting in the car downstairs and I really have to get going or she's going to kill me."

"Sorry Steve, but you and I both know that Karen's pretty understanding about things like this." Steven begrudgingly nodded in agreement. "But this is all I have for the front page. Simkin didn't come through on his piece, and frankly what you have is better than his assignment anyway. I don't have a front page if you don't do this, and if you don't do this you don't have a job. It's as simple as that. We already have the space set aside – we just need you to fill in the blanks."

"It's Steven, not Steve, Fred." Steven reminded him. "And what the hell happened to Simkin's story? I mean … come on." Steven paused and took a breath. "What I'm saying here is you have to give me more time if you want something like you're asking for. If you're only going to give me a few hours notice, you might as well have me write a short little whatever to throw in some back page of the paper. This is frankly, pardon my French, bullshit. Karen's waiting in the car downstairs and I honestly don't have time to waste on this."

"Steven? What's taking so long?" Karen leaned her head around the door to Fred's office. "Are we going to get going here or what? I've been waiting in the car for like fifteen minutes already."

"Karen, honey, you go ahead home," said Fred, glaring at Steven. "Steven is going to be a while. I need him to revise his story so we can run it as the lead in tomorrow's paper." Fred knew Steven wanted a job, and there wasn't anywhere else in Courtsdale that would hire him, not on Steven's terms at least. There was no question Steven would write the story.

Steven returned the glare, and turned to face Karen. "I'm really sorry Hun. I have to do this; you know how it goes. Just take the car home; I'll catch a cab after I'm done here."

Karen grabbed the keys from Steven's hand. "You know what Steven? I can't take this anymore. Fuck it. I'll talk to you later. Don't expect me to be there when you get home."

Not wanting to cause any more of a scene in front of his boss than Fred had already seen, Steven turned back to face him, ignoring Karen's comments.

"Fuck you Steven. Fuck you."

And with that she left the office, slamming the door on the way out.

Fred was the first to break the silence. "Steven? The story?"

"Yeah. I'll have it for you soon."

"Good, you can use Simkin's computer if you want. I'm pretty sure he's gone for the day."

Nine

It was well past eleven o' clock by the time Steven finally wandered into his apartment. Countless revisions and a generally pissed-off attitude had taken their toll on his spirit. This, coupled with the fact Karen kept her word and was nowhere to be seen upon his return, further solidified the reality that Steven's day had not ended as he had hoped it would.

Mr. Stinky met him at the door, brushing up against Steven's tired legs as he entered the apartment. "Not now Banky. Go play with your mouse, or something."

"Miaow?" Banky questioned. As a cat, he didn't care much about Steven's day. All he cared about was getting some much needed petting. There was an itch behind his ears that, try as he might, he had been unable to scratch the entire day.

"No! Get out of here you little bastard." Steven kicked Banky out of his way with his foot, causing him to let out a small yelp.

After a slow amble to the kitchen, Steven grabbed what was left of last evening's vodka and headed to the couch. Banky leapt onto the couch and nestled into Steven's lap. Steven, who was too beat and depressed, abandoned the fight and gave into Banky's demands.

"Hey there Mr. Stinky," he sighed. "Why does she have to be so difficult all the time? She's just a stupid daycare worker. She has no idea what it's like to have a job with demands and responsibility. All she does is watch kids all day long and feels like she's making a difference. Anyone could do her job – it's nowhere near as important as what I do. You'd think she'd realize that.... Why am I talking to you anyway? You're just a cat..."

Steven looked down to the bottle in his right hand. Only a few minutes earlier it had been half full. All that remained now was one last drink. Steven lifted the bottle and finished it off. He didn't even hear the crack of his head as it hit the wooden arm of his couch.

Day Two

CONTROL[2]

[2]Play Audio: "Personal Jesus" by Depeche Mode

the trouble with being god

Ten

He slowly slid his hand upon the bare skin at the nape of her neck, feeling her body tremble slightly. His fingertips sensed every pulse of blood as they wandered down to the small of her back just below her naked left shoulder. Her skin, soft and tender to the touch, shook at each simple stroke as his frozen hands met her warmth. She felt their chill hovering above her body as they disturbed the air above her skin whenever they ventured near, before eventually shying away, teasing her.

His head turned to the side and he placed his left cheek to her wavering lips, the tiny bristles on his chin stirring in unison with their trembling. He could hear her whispering, pleading, "Please… please let me go."

He felt the wetness on his cheek as a lone tear fell from her eye.

"Please." She whispered again, her mind so gripped by panic that the words struggled against her tongue. "Please don't do this." Her body began to shake more, both from the coldness of the bare concrete floor as well as from her fear. He smiled as he felt another of her tears meet his cheek.

His hand brushed cross her neck, gently caressing her sweet pale skin. With a small razor nestled between his middle and ring fingers he began cutting. It was just a slight flesh wound, barely a scratch - just enough to draw a trickle of blood. Her eyes confessed her desire to scream, but the gun in his other hand, pressed firmly against her left temple, stifled this craving.

He ran his tongue along her neck. Once. Twice. The salt of her sweat thrilled his appetite.

Then, with a forceful stroke of the blade, the serious cutting began - his tongue following close behind to taste the weight of her blood. In short time, however, even this composure gave way to rancor and his impatient hand plunged the razor deep into her throat.

She tried again to scream, but was left with nothing but a gurgle. The blood gushed from the gash in her windpipe and he quickly moved aside to avoid being stained by the cascade. Missing him completely, it spilt over her naked body, down across her breasts, smacking wetly onto the bare concrete. As the outpouring subsided it gave way to a few throaty gurgles, until it was nothing but a pulsing trickle.

The previously cold concrete was now wet and hot with her blood. It flowed along the floor, filling each individual crack along its journey. He marveled at the sight of the event, lost in wonderment as the blood continued to spill. A smile crept across his face and the razor dropped from his hand onto her chest, before tumbling to the floor washed red with blood. He felt strangely vacant, dreamlike, his senses overloaded. As he slowly licked his fingers clean his gaze returned to the face of the woman before him. Her pleading eyes turned back in the head. Up towards the sky. And Steven awoke with a start.

His sheets clung to his body, drenched with sweat. On the night stand stood a glass of water, which he consumed in a single drink. The clock read 8:29, it was earlier than he usually woke but Steven decided he may as well get up and shower. He still had never been able to fall back asleep, even after all the nights he'd been woken from this particular nightmare.

The cramped shower offered little refuge from Steven's dream world, yet the warmth of the water against his naked skin was comforting. He couldn't be quite sure when the dreams had started, but what he was certain of was that they were repeating themselves. They had begun with a barrage of images in his mind each night as he closed his eyes to sleep. The sights would flash across his thoughts and at first he had been unable to make them out. It was a mental attack; the machine-gun fire of thoughts was seen yet not processed. They were not pleasant thoughts.

After some time the flashes began to transform into cohesive thoughts, and then into dreams. For over a month now, Steven could remember nothing but dreams of darkness. Each night the dream was different from the night before. And, at first he couldn't recall much more than the general feel of the dream along with a few images which could be translated into a simple, yet gruesome story. These were hateful dreams – dreams of stabs with garden trowels, skulls beaten in with shovels or golf clubs, and most recently, cutting with razor blades.

Until recently the dreams hadn't shown any kind of pattern other than the gruesomeness of the acts and a memory of standing above the bloody beaten body, harboring a sense of triumph. Again, this was until recently. Now each night the dream had begun to repeat itself: always with the girl on the concrete floor. Dead and bloodied on the concrete floor, by his own hands. She didn't appear to be any girl in particular – just a girl. Steven never even managed to look at her face. During his dream he thought it better that way. If he didn't look, he wouldn't care. It added mystery and furthered the enjoyment.

But each time the dream came he was woken from it. And upon waking it wasn't joy that he felt, but disgust.

Now, as he felt the tepid water run across his face he couldn't help but be reminded of the dream. He looked to the shower floor as he wet his hair, half expecting to see not water flowing below his feet but the girl's streaming blood. The water circling the drain was pink. He gagged and pressed his eyelids shut.

"No… there is no way that there is blood in here, it was just a dream." Steven's eyes remained shut as he repeated this through his head.

Upon opening his eyes, he was met with the sight of blood flowing in the water below, causing him to rush from the shower and vomit in the toilet. It was only then that he felt a sharp pain in his right foot. He reached his hand to his foot and retrieved a bloody shard of glass from his sole. The pain from the cut was insignificant compared to the relief he felt in discovering the blood's source. Karen must have missed some of the bottle when she cleaned the shower the night before.

Thank God she didn't step on this, she would have been crying about it all night long, Steven thought as he heard the shard clink against the side of the garbage can.

Even though he was sure he had disposed of the source of his shower terror, he reached in and turned off the water. He wasn't about to go back in the shower this morning; the images remained all too fresh in his head.

Steven pulled on his flannel boxers and a pair of worn blue jeans. Looking up at the mirror, he wiped its layer of steam condensation clear and took a step back.

It was true: he *had* seen better days, but his current profile still in no way reflected the mental battle going on inside. He lifted his hand to his chin and felt the rough stubble of a man who hadn't shaved in days. He moved closer again, looking deep into his own bottomless blue eyes. They had begun to sink the last week or so and were now harbor to an ominous darkness.

His hair was dyed a muddy brown – that nearly black color of potting soil, minus the little white Styrofoam balls. Just a few months earlier his hair had been shaved close to his scalp, but now he decided to let it grow out a bit. It was still wet from the shower and looked a bit messy, but this is how it would end up looking later in the day. As it dried it would take on a slight curl and would look well enough without much management, as it was still only just over two inches in length.

Steven stepped forward and placed both hands upon the sides of his sink. He lowered his head until his forehead met the mirror, and stared deeper – past his eyes. He hadn't actually looked at himself, other than in passing, for several days. His own reflection now looked like that of a stranger.

"Who the hell am I?"

It was a question that went deeper than the mirror allowed. He took in a deep breath and let it out, fogging the mirror up again. He pulled back his head and splashed a bit of cold water onto his face. His reflection was muddled with steam; except for the clearing where his forehead had been, protected from the mist of his exhale.

"Now, where did I put my razor…?"

A soft meow from outside the bathroom door was the only reply. Steven's heart froze at the unexpected realization that he felt terribly alone.

Eleven

Two train delays and a three-car accident first put Steven in Darlington at a few minutes past ten o' clock. The drive, which normally took him only twenty minutes out of the city through a stretch of quaint country roads, instead took nearly an hour. The weather had again turned to shit, and in place of country charm Steven was forced to endure beleaguered traffic and an extensive detour around Mill Creek Road, whose bridge had apparently washed out in last week's storms.

St. Mary's Church had been built around the turn of the century, and while historic in its own right was a blossom of youth compared to its neighbors. Darlington was one of the original settlements in the area and had once been a burgeoning town on the brink of city-dom. This was until the abandonment of its railways in favor of the automobile. Courtsdale, born at the intersection of Kettleman's Bay and the freshly reconstructed interstate attracted most of Darlington's initial population and over the past fifteen-or-so years Darlington became suburb to the new lake-side metropolis. In spite of this shift of populace, however, Darlington retained its historic architecture and celebrated its roots and "country values." As such, preservation was of great importance, and the majority of the town lingered upon its faltering 19th Century foundations. St. Mary's Church was new in comparison, its rebirth born out of the ashes from the 1894 fire.

The church's simplistic design gave the town a sense of completion, making it the postcard-perfect lake town. White slat-board walls reached up from a base built of concrete and fieldstones gathered from nearby farms during the town's infancy.

Steven followed up the concrete steps, running his hand lightly along the black wrought iron railing. He felt the chill of cold metal in the places where the paint had worn from years of devout churchgoers, those souls in need of answers and direction.

The church had seen countless occasions of joy as well as despair, and its members always looked to it and its teachings to give meaning to both.

As he reached the last step, cracked with knowledge, his eye caught a stained-glass representation of the Virgin Mary set in the façade above the church's double oak doors. He'd been here before with Karen, and he'd seen it all countless times before. Only this time he took the time to really look around. It was a building to him – nothing more and nothing less. This time, however, he realized this creature of stone and wood was more to some other people.

"Poor, misguided souls," Steven muttered as he pushed open the heavy oak door.

Despite its outward appearance, the church's interior opened up to a great expanse. Rows of wooden pews were laid out before him – fifteen, possibly twenty on each side. It was enough to accommodate the church-goers in town, the stragglers who came in from outlying areas, and even the occasional member of the congregation who just couldn't let go of his or her roots – despite the fact that they'd abandoned Jesus in favor of the city years ago.

Ahead in the first pew Steven saw Sister Katherine kneeling down, her head lowered in prayer. As he stepped forward to make his way to the front of the church he paused in hesitation, then took a step backward, dipped his hand in the marble font of holy water and genuflected, pantomiming the sign of the cross. It was a motion of routine more than anything else, his Catholic upbringing still ingrained in parts of his behavior. Besides, Steven thought, it would appear disrespectful if he simply ignored the "spirituality" of the place, and he wanted as much cooperation from Sister Katherine as possible. Any unneeded tension would surely not help his chances of getting a good interview, much less getting any comments at all.

"Excuse me, Sister Katherine?"

Sister Katherine quickly made the Sign of the Cross and whispered a quiet prayer before raising her eyes to meet Steven. As they connected, Steven sensed a hollow sadness entrenched in hers. A deep green sea of emptiness was spread out before him, wet with the precursors to tears. Sister Katherine had either been crying earlier or he had interrupted her just prior to breakdown. Either way, Steven would have to choose his words carefully to avoid any unfortunate incidents. He had neither the time nor the patience to deal with an emotionally distressed nun.

"Sister Katherine, I'm Steven Carvelle, from the *Courtsdale Courier*. I think we may have met briefly at the Coroner's Office in town yesterday."

Immediately after saying this, Steven knew he had made a mistake. He shouldn't have even mentioned yesterday, at least not until the interview. Now he had pulled up even more memories she had no doubt only recently begun to displace. Steven coughed slightly and hurried back into conversation, hoping the sudden change of tone would keep her from even comprehending his previous comment.

"Well, anyway, I called over yesterday and was unable to reach you. I was wondering if you had a few minutes to talk."

"Mr. Carvelle," she began, her voice thick from the choke of sorrow, "I don't especially want to talk, but if it means you will leave me alone sooner, rather than later, I'll answer your questions."

Steven had met Sister Katherine many years earlier when he and Karen first started dating. In the beginning Karen had insisted Steven come to church with her, regardless of whether it meant anything to him or not. For Karen, the Church had always been a significant part of her life and she needed the person she cared about to be along for her experience. She had no intentions of forcing religion upon Steven; her reasons for asking him along were for her own personal gratification. What she wanted was for Steven to be there beside her, in that place that meant so much. It was simply enough for her that he came along.

It was during one of these visits to St. Mary's, many years earlier, that Sister Katherine had stopped Karen as she was leaving the church. Steven had been walking (rushing, Karen would contend) out of the church at the end of service, pulling Karen in tow. Just as he was about to cross the threshold to the somewhat saner world outside, he felt a tug from Karen indicating their sudden stop in departure.

"And who is this young man?" he heard as he turned his head back toward Karen. He looked to the side and was met with the reason for their detain, a little woman withered with age, but still extending a youthful strength of confidence and spry energy.

"Oh this old thing?" said Karen, grinning at Steven, knowingly poking at his contempt for being referred to as old. "This is Steven, Sister Katherine." As she turned her head back to Sister Katherine, she couldn't help but let out a giddy smile along with a look Sister Katherine correctly translated as a blissful *I think he's the one!*

"Well hello there, Steven." This time, upon opening her mouth, Steven noticed she was missing two or three teeth – an incisor a molar, maybe a bicuspid. He couldn't be certain, as his comprehension was suddenly knocked off track by the sour smell Steven could only assume emanated from within her lungs.

Steven responded only with an impatient smile and a slight wave of his hand, keeping his mouth shut to avoid any contact with this foul aroma. Sister Katherine sensed his contempt, and pushed it aside hoping for even a bit of trite conversation.

"Karen?" Steven questioned impatiently, gesturing his head toward the door. "Shall we?"

Karen sensed his impertinence, and letting out a small huff said goodbye to Sister Katherine. "Well, I guess we have to get going. I'll talk to you later, Sister."

"Goodbye Karen. It was nice meeting you Steven. You two behave now!" Her attempt at a wink to the couple came out as a bizarre face contortion, reminding Steven of the homeless guy on Fourth Street with the nervous twitch. And while Karen seemed not to notice and gave a smile in return, Steven exhibited a look of disgust as he turned once again to finally leave. It was the last time Steven came to church with Karen.

Now, years later, Steven noticed time had been less than kind to Sister Katherine. The withered woman from before was now not much more than a walking wrinkle, and the reek of her breath had aged as sourly as a fine cheese. Still, Steven disregarded this as best he could so as to further his own cause. The sooner he asked his questions, the sooner he could get out of this damned place.

"So, Sister Katherine, how long have you known Father Bergens?"

Twelve

"Oh God - what time is it?" Karen moaned, combating the sun from her eyes. The blinds in her apartment were still open; she hadn't thought of closing them in her drunken awkwardness the night before. Now, waking from a night of dreams she would never recall, her hands moved in a tired attempt to push the light from her face. She groaned again, pulling her red flannel sheets up above her head as she turned to bury her face into the soft down of her pillow.

"Oh fuck." Karen sat up with a start, knocking a bag of microwave popcorn off the bed to the floor. *Damn, damn, damn. I can't believe I overslept!* she thought.

It wasn't until she made these sudden movements that she realized her body was aching from an extreme hangover, brought on by last night's activities. Preoccupied with thoughts of being late for work four times in the same month, Karen quickly brushed the remaining popcorn kernels from her sheets onto the floor. They'd be much easier to vacuum up when she got home and there was no reason to stain her sheets with popcorn butter. She glanced towards the clock: 8:30 a.m., only thirty minutes until work and she *had* to shower. The kids wouldn't appreciate the smell of cigarettes and alcohol currently permeating her body and hair.

"Oh screw it. There's no way in hell I'm going to be able to take a shower and still get to work on time… let's just hope Angela doesn't come in today." Angela, Karen's boss, was generally an understanding woman. She had recently, however, begun to tire of Karen's frequent tardiness and general projection of malaise at the work place. Karen had already been late three times in October, which wouldn't have been the biggest deal, had Karen not taken the first week off for vacation and been late for three of the seven days she had worked since.

So, after weighing the option of smelling like a boozehound against the chances of getting her sorry ass fired for making Beverly watch thirty kids all by her lonesome, Karen decided to go for the hat instead. She rushed to the closet, threw on a pair of worn blue jeans, a tight green T-shirt, and her time-torn Boston Red Sox hat. The plastic adjuster had broken after years of use, and was now held together by a thick bundle of duct tape.

Karen looked to the mirror, checking out her rag-tag ensemble. *Damn, I'm still cute as hell*, she thought to herself, grinning. She flipped the light switch off and stepped out the door.

Work went on as any other workday: the children cried, she came to their rescue, they loved her, then five minutes after she walked away they cried again – at least that's how Karen saw it. She had made it to work in time, with a full twenty-five seconds to spare. And although she hadn't had her morning latté, she was feeling surprisingly well. Her headache had subsided on the drive to work, and other than the fact that her body felt disgustingly dirty, everything was good.

The eleven o' clock hour was nearing, a time she normally reserved for her cigarette break. Yet, even though she was feeling much better, even the simple *thought* of a cigarette in her mouth sent her stomach lurching. Besides, she thought, she should probably call Steven to let him know she was alright. Not that he cared; he didn't give a shit about her lately it seemed. There was no call from him the night before asking where she was and no call in the morning to see how she was doing. She hadn't heard from him since she left him at the office. And, even though she had been the one to leave, it was his job as a man to give in and call her up and apologize for ditching out on their plans.

"Screw him. If he is going to be a prick about this and not call, then screw him. I'm not calling his sorry ass. Let him sit there and suffer. It will do him good." Karen needed to tell herself these things. Beverly had convinced her of this over lunch last Thursday.

"Hun, if you're not happy with how things are going, you have to take matters into your own hands. You treat him like he's your everything – always doing whatever it is Steven wants to do and all that. You used to have a life – you used to *smile*. Now you're turning into this ragged old bitch, a cute ragged old bitch, but a bitch nonetheless. Give him some shit to deal with himself, let him know that you aren't going to put up with it. It's your right as a woman." Beverly, herself, was single. She hadn't had a steady boyfriend in over three years, and was usually the last person Karen looked to for dating advice. Still, she did have a point. Karen *wasn't* happy with how things had been lately and it had begun to affect her personal relationships as well. So, for once she listened to what Beverly had to say and took a new proactive approach to her life.

So, instead of calling Steven, Karen opted to sit down with a cup of coffee and a copy of Wednesday's *Courier*. It was then that she saw what it was that had kept Steven from going out the night before. Her eyes locked on a photograph of Father Bergens. It filled half the front page of the paper. Her eyes scanned to the headline:

Local Priest Killed in Execution-Style Murder

"Oh… my… God," Karen gasped aloud. Thoughts tripped through her brain like blowing fuses, stumbling then firing upon one another as she fought to gain comprehension of what lay before her. It was there in unmistakable black and white, yet she could hardly believe it. Most of all she couldn't believe Steven had kept this from her. She blinked her eyes and returned them to the page; it was his story sure enough, "by Steven Carvelle," read the byline.

As her mind dissected the words, tears welled up in her eyes, dripping onto the paper. The picture of Father Bergens became stained with her tears, the ink of his smile bleeding into the jumble of letters before her. She understood the sentences, yet they spoke of nonsense. Father Bergens was not dead - there was no way. And even if he was dead, the acts spoken of in the paper just didn't happen. These were scenes from a sick movie; things like this didn't happen in real life. Things like this didn't happen to people you *knew*.

It was only after she finished forcing herself to read the article that she realized why Steven hadn't told her about what had happened. What had happened was pure nonsense - a nonsensical reality. There was no way Steven could have broken this news to her personally, though it tore her heart that it had to be so.

Still fighting back her tears, Karen reached for the phone. Her little games seemed stale now and she needed to talk to Steven – if only to find comfort in the sound of his voice.[3]

---

[3]Play Audio: "Starlings" by Elbow

Thirteen

"Be sure that you have me down for two tonight, Ms. Winfreid. … That's correct, a guest and me. … I told you this before; I told you I would be bringing a guest. … No Ms. Winfreid. … Never you mind who I'm bringing, that's my personal business. Now, as I said, be sure there is a place at the head table for both my guest and myself…"

John Paluniak's corner office at Liberty Mutual overlooked Braidwood Ravine and the Carten River flowing through it. Not the grandest of rivers, the Carten was relatively narrow: no more than fifteen feet across at its widest. Still, it was a beautiful view, especially in the autumn. The turning leaves decorating the twisted arms of the oaks and maples that lined the river's edge were at their most beautiful this time of the season. They had just begun to fall, garnishing the crawling river's surface with bursts of reds and oranges.

Some days, as John looked down at the river below, it was as if a sunset were flowing beneath him. Today, however, the river ambled along sadly as mists of rain settled upon it. The gray sky above cast no reflection in the water. Braidwood Ravine appeared sullen and lifeless.

"How many times must I repeat myself?" John sighed. "Two. … No, not just me – that would be one. Two. Thank you Ms. Winfreid, I'll see you later tonight. … Goodbye Ms. Winfreid."

John reached across his desk and clicked off his speakerphone. Rather than take a seat at his desk, he returned to the window. As he neared the window, he stretched his arms above his head and placed his palms and forehead against the cool double-paned glass. John Paluniak, widowed husband of Shawna and father of Dakota pressed his eyelids shut and breathed an exhausted sigh.

There were times when it was all John could do to not think about Shawna, to not see her face every place he looked. He had worked for years to get over the grief he felt for his loss, for both his and Dakota's loss. Having never known his mother, Dakota had been raised by John alone. Now, as he stood in his corner office on the twenty-third floor of the Liberty Building, he struggled to bring forth the memories of Shawna. Over the years many memories had been buried in frustration, but many more had dissolved with time. Still, every time he closed his eyes he could still smell her hair, still taste her lips, and still feel the warmth he felt when she whispered into his ear *I love you*.

On days like today, and nights like this night, John ached to bring back more feelings and more memories. It was because of Shawna and the heart complications that led to her death during Dakota's childbirth that John had become whom he had. In the years since, John had continued to strive for success in his work to ensure Dakota would have a happy life. In the years since, John had worked just as hard to keep other families from suffering as he and Dakota had.

John had become a member of the American Heart Disease Awareness and Treatment Association's (AHDATA) volunteer association shortly after Dakota's birth (and Shawna's death). His knowledge and experience in financial matters, along with his tight ties to the community, had propelled him forward in the ranks of the Heart Association as well. And in these few years, become the acting president of the Courtsdale division of AHDATA.

Tonight the yearly charity gala for AHDATA would take place at the Hotel Paramount in downtown Courtsdale. It was a $3,000 a plate dinner and all proceeds would go to AHDATA. And, while it was far from the only fundraising effort AHDATA ran, it had become one of the most essential benefits financially. On top of this, due in large part to AHDATA's community presence, the AHDATA Gala had also become one of, if not *the* most prestigious social event of the season.

As John thought about this and how much things had changed in the time since Shawna he once again smelt her hair and felt the warmth of her skin. A tear dropped from his eye onto the floor below and John opened his eyes to the valley below. The rain had subsided and he caught a glimpse of the sun reflecting off the water below as it began to peek through the cheerless clouds above.[4]

---

[4]Play Audio: "I See Monsters" by Ryan Adams

Fourteen

"Where am I now? I'm downtown, but I'll be leaving here soon. I'm heading over to Stengler again to check things out – make sure everything is under control there. God knows we don't want another incident like we had with the Telbert case."

"Back to Stengler, huh? Well I'm on my way back to town, myself. Stengler's not really that much out of the way for me. Think I could meet you there, Miles? I'd like to catch up with you about the case so far."

"Yeah, that sounds fine Steve. I won't be there for another half-hour or so though, so you might have to wait around for me. That cool with you?"

"Yeah that's fine. I'll probably be there in about ten. Oh yeah - one quick question."

"What's that?"

"Do you really think there's going to be a frenzy going on outside the brewery? I'd really rather not have to deal with that."

"You should know; they're your people."

Steven turned onto the off-ramp for downtown Courtsdale as he flipped his portable phone closed. The windows to his silver Civic were cracked open, letting a flow of the cool outside air fill the vehicle. The rain had subsided while he was inside St. Mary's church interviewing Sister Katherine. Now the sun had begun to filter through the clouds above, giving rise to small clouds of steam born from the wet streets of downtown Courtsdale.

Steven rolled the driver's-side window down the rest of the way and took a deep breath of the crisp air outside. Despite the sun, the air still held a chill; and the bite Steven felt within his lungs ensured he was at his most awake state.

He looked down to the clock on his stereo. It was eleven o' clock. His interview with Sister Katherine had gone on longer than he had hoped but shorter than he had feared. The rest of the day would be a cakewalk in comparison.

Eleven o' clock and already the worst of the day is over. Steven thought to himself as he looked up into the clearing sky. *Finally we're going to have a beautiful day.*

Steven's smile faded from his face as he pulled his car to the curb next to the alley behind the brewery. The entire alley had been taped off by police and was still marked as a crime scene. The police had no doubt already finished up with the majority of their initial investigation, but given the nature of the crime it was in their best interest to keep things as protected as possible. The police tape, however, was not the reason for Steven's frown.

In front of the police tape were several news vans and dozens of reporters, each of whom dreamt of getting the next big scoop on the story. Steven hated these people. They were sensationalists; they didn't care about getting the real story. All they cared about was entertaining their audience with true-life tales of horror and misery – all garnished with a tasteless emotional edge, courtesy of the editors. These were the people he had gone to school with, had trained with, and been forced to work with. They were also the reason Steven did his best to keep away from the office and do his work on his own schedule and his own ethics.

"Oh Christ," Steven groaned as he clicked off the car's ignition. Unfastening his seatbelt, he took a deep breath to prepare himself for the possible confrontations that lie ahead. Mary Tremel from Channel Four News was just ahead of him; he hoped he hadn't been spotted.

Just as he was about to get out of the car and enter the jungle before him, his phone rang. Steven's eyes continued to stare forward as he flipped the phone open, answering the incoming call.

"You on your way here or what, Miles?" said Steven. "It's a zoo out here."

"Who the *fuck* do you think you are, Steven? I can't believe the shit you pull sometimes. The least you could have done was told me so I didn't have to find out the news in the paper today!"

Steven rolled his eyes, restraining the groan erupting inside. *I don't need this shit, not now,* Steven thought to himself. *God, I'd rather be dealing with that Tremel bitch than this.*

"I'm sorry Karen. I was going to tell you about it after we got home from our night out last night. I wasn't trying to keep it a secret damn it, I just wanted us to be able to have a good time. God knows you would have been an emotional mess if I'd told you earlier in the night. There was nothing you could do about it; what was done was done. I wasn't about to let your chick emotions ruin a good evening."

"You asshole! You total asshole! Don't you give a shit about how I feel?" Karen's voice trembled with fury. "I've known Father Bergens for as long as I can remember, and you don't even have the *balls* to tell me he's been killed? You are such a shit."

Steven was more annoyed than upset. Karen had accused him of being an asshole before. Actually she had accused him of being more than that: asshole, jerk, bastard, blah, blah, blah; Steven had learned to ignore the name calling. It wasn't the name calling that was annoying him, not even the fact that she was upset with him. What was annoying Steven was the fact that at this moment he had more important things to do than talk to her.

"Listen. I said I was sorry, what more do you want? I was going to tell you. You were just in such a good mood last night; I didn't want to ruin it ... I'm pretty certain that telling you would have ruined it."

"Whatever. I can't believe how insensitive you are sometimes. You don't even care about my feelings."

"Oh, would you just quit with the theatrics already? There's nothing I can do to change what I did. I said I'm sorry and that's all I can do."

Well he does have a point there, conceded Karen. Arguing with him wasn't going to get any results, other than act as a vent for her frustration and sadness at the news. "Alright fine, Steven. So, have you learned anything else? I mean, besides what's in the papers?"

Thank you Jesus, she's finally calming down.

"No, I haven't really learned much of anything. I did head out to St. Mary's this morning to talk to Sister Katherine, but she didn't have much to say other than what I already knew. Oh yeah, that reminds me, she wanted me to say hello to you and let you know that she'll let you know when services are going to take place. I'm actually down at Stengler again right now, waiting for Miles to show up so I can find out what else he's learned. Damn Tremel is down here too, along with the rest of the city's press; God, I hate that bitch. I can let you know what I find out after I get home tonight."

"Yeah, fine, Steven, that's nice. Well thanks for the message from Sister Katherine. Hopefully that didn't go too badly; I know you don't like her all that much."

Steven almost replied, but decided it was best to disregard that comment.

"And about tonight, I won't be able to see you – I have plans."

"Plans? What plans? You didn't tell me anything about plans for Wednesday night. What are you doing? Going out with the girls from work? You know I can't stand that Beverly. She's nothing but trouble. I don't think-"

"Well I don't particularly *care* what you think, Steven," interrupted Karen. "Besides, I'm not going out with her or anyone from the daycare. I promised John Paluniak I'd go with him to the AHDATA gala thing tonight."

"What the *fuck*, Karen. Why are you going with John to that thing?" Steven didn't get jealous often, but he wore his jealousy on his sleeve when it came to John Paluniak. "And when did you talk to him? I'd think you would have told me about this sooner – or were you hoping that you could go without me knowing?"

"Oh would you just quit it Steven?" Karen's patience was beginning to wear thin. "He needed someone to go along with him and hadn't found a date yet so I said I'd do it as a friend. He *is* my friend, Steven."

"Fine. But you still didn't tell me when you saw him. How long have you had these plans? Jesus Karen, I'd think you could extend me at least a tiny bit of courtesy and let me know some of your plans."

"First of all, my plans are my plans. It's my life Steven. It's not like you and I are married or anything. And even if we were, there's no rule that says I need to tell you every little detail about my life. If you must know, however, he asked me last night. We went out to The Connection after you ditched me for your damn work."

"You went out with him for drinks? You fuck him as a nightcap?"

"Go to hell Steven," was Karen's soft reply before Steven heard the phone click.

That bitch hung up on me. Damn it, why does she do shit just to frustrate me? Steven's heart was racing and beads of sweat had formed on his brow. Luckily for Steven he had years of practice controlling his jealousy, things had gotten much, much worse in the past. That was no doubt the reason Karen had been reluctant to tell Steven about her plans with John Paluniak.

Steven first met Karen when he moved to Courtsdale after receiving his undergraduate degree in journalism from Georgetown back in 1988. Karen had received her education at Courtsdale Community College, where she earned her English degree and teaching certificate. It was also at CCC that she first met Shawna and John.

Shawna moved to Courtsdale from Chapel Hill, North Carolina to attend school at CCC. She didn't really have that much of a reason to come to Courtsdale, other than that she had family in the area. Her mother was originally from Courtsdale and had attended CCC herself back in the 1960s, but moved to Chapel Hill soon after graduation.

Shawna's grandparents had remained in Courtsdale after their retirement and offered Shawna a place to stay while she got herself settled in the area. She took them up on their offer, and spent her first year in Courtsdale living at their little brown townhouse on the corner of 22nd and Evergreen Terrace.

It was during this first year at CCC that Karen and Shawna met. Both girls joined the freshman intramural soccer team, and instantly became close friends. After the first year had come to an end the two girls decided to get an apartment together near campus. Karen had grown jaded to living with her parents and Shawna was feeling a need to finally get out on her own. So the two of them gathered together what belongings they had and found a ramshackle two-bedroom apartment in the Ridgestone Apartments off Juniper St.

During their third year at Triple-C Karen met John while leaving the library one Sunday night. Karen had just finished writing her mid-term essay for Eighteenth Century English Literature and was walking back to her apartment when, upon turning the corner of 6th and Juniper, she was nearly broad-sided by a man riding a bike on the sidewalk in the opposite direction.

"Are you okay?" The man had stopped his bike suddenly; skidding on the wet concrete after realizing he had just missed knocking Karen to the ground. "I didn't hurt you did I?"

"No, I'm fine – just a bit shaken," came the rattled reply. "You really should slow down and watch where you're going."

"Here, let me help you with those." The man got off his bike and pointed to Karen's papers littering the sidewalk.

"No, that's not necessary. I can take care of …" Karen's voice trailed off as the man moved toward her, his face illuminating in the light of the street lamp nearest her. "Actually, yeah, if you could give me a hand that would be so nice of you."

Karen couldn't help but smile at the stranger, seeing as how she found him absolutely gorgeous. He looked perfect: short black hair, solid body, well dressed, and a deep resonating voice. *I think I'm in love*, Karen mused.

"Hey, I'm really sorry about that. I guess I do need to take my time and slow down once in a while," the man said as he knelt down and began to gather Karen's papers. "My name's John, by the way."

"I'm Karen, it's nice to meet you," she said as she too knelt down and shook his hand. *Wow, what strong hands. God, this is too much... keep yourself under control, girl.*

"Well Karen, I'm pleased to meet you as well. It's too bad we had to meet under these circumstances. I don't normally try to run pretty girls off the road, you know." John grinned as he said this. "Anyway, I have to get going. You're sure you aren't hurt or anything?"

"Hurt? No, not hurt… I guess I'll be fine."

"Well, where were you going? I'm on my way up Juniper; do you live around here?" John sensed a letdown in Karen's voice and figured he might as well be a gentleman. "If you do, I'd be happy to walk you home," he offered with a smile.

"Oh you don't have to do that… but if you want to, I won't argue." Karen was doing her best to refrain from turning her face into one tremendous grin. "I actually live on Juniper, just up the street here. If you want to walk me there and protect me from any more dangerous bikers, I'd be honored."

As the two walked down the street, Karen did her best to keep from staring at John. Her immediate infatuation did not go unnoticed however, and John found himself instantly interested in discovering more about this young lady. In less than five minutes the two had reached the entrance for Karen's apartment building. She hated to say goodbye, as she had just met John, and was just about to ask him if she could have his number (something Karen rarely did), when John spoke.

"You live here? This is actually where I'm going. Hold just a second." Karen waited at the door, fumbling with her keys all the while trying her best to hide her excitement at meeting such a gorgeous and apparently intelligent man. "Think you could let me in? I'm stopping in to visit my … um," John paused briefly, "my friend – she lives in Apartment 108. Maybe you know her? Her name's Shawna Kenmer."

Karen's heart dropped at the mention of Apartment 108 and Shawna. "So *this* is that John who Shawna's been talking about nonstop. Well it's typical I guess – I meet someone and my friend steals him from me. At least she could have done me the courtesy of waiting to steal him until *after* I had gotten the chance to go out with him once or twice."

"Yeah I know Shawna." Karen heaved a disappointed sigh. "I live in Apartment 108 too – I'm Shawna's roommate. 108 Juniper Street, that's my address too." Karen noticed the frustration in her own voice and, in an attempt to hide her let down, added, "Come on, and follow me. I'll even let you in so you don't have to wait out here in the rain." Karen opened the door and looked at John, who himself looked taken aback by the coincidence. "Hurry up John, I don't have all day," Karen added only half-joking.

In the months that followed, John and Shawna began dating. The dating eventually gave blossom to a relationship, a relationship Karen couldn't help but be jealous of. While Shawna was dating someone who was the epitome of a perfect man, Karen had been left to fend for herself in the bars and clubs of Courtsdale. On more than one occasion she had woken up in the bed of a strange man, or had been forced to kick a strange man out of her own bed in the unclouded realization of a sober morning. Shawna wasn't oblivious to Karen's jealousy, but there was little she could do about it other than console Karen with the belief that one day her prince would come as well.

During this time the three also grew to become good friends. John would stay up late at night talking with Karen, sharing hopes and dreams of what the future may hold. One night, however, Karen could no longer hold back her feelings and felt it necessary to expose her feelings for John.

The three had been out at Bella's Café enjoying a generous selection of drinks to celebrate the end of the first semester of their senior year. Somehow, through what must have been a combination of teamwork and a miracle, the three compatriots managed to wander their way back to Karen and Shawna's apartment safely. As soon as they got into the apartment, Shawna loudly announced she was headed for bed. John and Karen both sat on the couch, laughing to themselves at Shawna's condition.

"Hey Shawna, are you alright honey? Are you going to make it bed all right? Or am I going to have to come in there to make sure you don't fall over before you make it to the bed?" John looked to Karen, to Shawna, then back to Karen and let out a stifled laugh.

"I'm going to sleep John. Why don't you get in here?" Shawna sputtered.

"I'll be there in a bit, I'm going to watch a bit of TV and drink some water so I don't get as bad of a hangover as you're going to have."

All this while Karen remained on the couch, watching the drama unfold. She did her best to hold back her laughter, but here and there a snicker would break free.

"That's cool. I'll be waiting for you though," Shawna said before slamming the door shut.

"She sure can't hold her liquor well," said Karen. "For the few years that I've known her, she's never been able to handle more than a few drinks before getting all messed up. I stopped telling her she needs to slow down – mostly because she doesn't listen, but also because it's just funny as heck when she gets sloshed."

"Yeah, I've noticed that about her," said John. "Maybe I need to get myself a woman who can handle her alcohol?" John added jokingly.

Karen turned her head and reseated herself to face John more directly. She hadn't noticed the flippancy in John's comment and, in her own state of alcohol-induced mental disillusion, took this to possibly be her chance to sway John to see something more than friendship in her. But rather than act impulsively, Karen still had enough wits about her to ease into the subject – to make her move with polish.

"You said you wanted a glass of water right? I'll go get us both one – I don't want a killer hangover either," Karen offered. "God, I'm going to laugh my butt off tomorrow when Shawna is stumbling around the apartment with her baggy eyes and frumpy hair," she added, before getting up from the couch and walking to the kitchen.

"Do you care what we watch?" John bellowed from his seat on the living room floor.

"No, turn on whatever you want. I don't particularly care." Karen yelled in return.

"Here you go sir, your water," Karen said, lowering her voice as she reentered the living room. She handed the glass to John and returned to the couch, seating herself directly behind him, nearly straddling his back with her knees.

"Here we go – Scooby Doo. Man, I remember watching these cartoons back when I was younger. I always loved this show."

"Geez John, the least you could do is say thank you," Karen joked, giving him a light slap to the back of his head. "Leave Scooby on, this shit is cool," Karen added, snickering.

After sitting a few minutes in a room full of silence, besides the sounds of the television, Karen placed her hands on John's shoulders and began massaging them. She kneaded her hands slowly on his tight muscles, all the while trying to decide if she should say anything or let her actions do the speaking while the perfect moment waited to present itself.

"Oh God that feels good, Karen. I've been so stressed out the last week, what with finals and all." John closed his eyes and began moving his head and upper body in motion with Karen's kneading: allowing himself to fully enjoy the pleasure. "You know, I'm really happy we got to know each other; you're really a cool girl."

"Shhhh," Karen whispered in his ear, moving her hands forward from his shoulders down to his chest. After a few minutes of silence from them both, she moved her hands back up to his neck, slowly tilting his head to the side. Slowly leaning forward, Karen placed her warm lips upon John's neck and proceeded to kiss him gently.

"Hold on a second, what are you doing?" asked John, brushing Karen's hands away. "Jesus Christ Karen, Shawna's in the next room. You know damn well she's my girlfriend, and she's your friend too. Don't even try this shit," he said, doing his best to retain his composure.

"I…I'm sorry John. I don't know what I was thinking. It must be the alcohol or something, I don't know," she said, attempting to disguise the hidden intentions behind the event.

"Sure Karen, you expect me to believe that? Christ – I know you're interested in me. It's not like you hide it that well or anything, and it's not like I'm not attracted to you either. The difference between you and me though is that you think it's okay to act on your animal instincts. I love Shawna, and there's nothing I would do to jeopardize that relationship. Nothing." John's heart was racing, but he managed to keep his voice relatively calm, mostly to avoid waking Shawna. "Now I'm going to assume that you've gotten this out of your system and we both know where I stand on the subject. I trust this won't happen again."

Karen looked up at John, who had risen to his feet to deliver his lecture. Tears welled in her eyes as he spoke down at her and she tried with all her might to fight them back. In the end, however, they escaped and Karen buried her face in the pile of pillows stacked at the end of the couch.

"Oh Karen, I'm not mad at you or anything," John said, taking a seat on the couch next to Karen. "I just want to make sure that everything goes good with all of us. We have a good thing going: you, me and

Shawna. You and I both know that. Let's just forget this happened, okay? Go back to being best friends again." John placed his hand on the back of Karen's head, rubbing her hair in an attempt at consolation. "It'll all be fine babe; trust me. Now you go get some sleep and everything will be back to normal in the morning."

From that night on Karen managed to keep her fantasies about John just that, fantasies. There were no more incidents, no more attempts to seduce her best friend's boyfriend. Neither mentioned the incident to Shawna, deciding it was best for the collective relationship if the little event was kept a secret.

Two year out of college, Karen still hadn't found a job satisfying her career hopes. She had taken up a job at a small daycare to earn some cash. Working at KinderKind necessitated working with children, something she had always enjoyed. Their playful exuberance and innocent sense of wonder fascinated Karen; working with children made her feel alive inside. It was a great job until she found something more suited to her education. Perhaps, she thought, working at a daycare for a few years would help get her foot in the door as a grade-school teacher at one of the local schools.

Karen had been working at KinderKind for only a few weeks when she met Steven. The two shared the same bus on the way to their respective jobs, and one day after seeing each other on the bus regularly they began to talk. One thing led to another and Steven asked Karen out to dinner and a movie. Eventually the two had formed a relationship, and during the formation of this relationship Steven was inevitably introduced to Karen's two best friends, John and Shawna, who were now engaged.

Steven was a relatively personable guy, when his arrogance didn't get the best of him, and he instantly became good friends with both John and Shawna. The four would double date often and other times they would just get together at one of their apartments for a night of drinking and board games.

After a few months of dating, Steven decided to ask Karen about her history with John and Shawna. It was a question he subconsciously didn't want to know the answer to, since he was fairly sure he already knew the answer yet didn't want to believe. And, even though Karen knew it might have been best to lie, she felt obliged to tell Steven the truth. After all, nothing had really happened between her and John; she had just wanted something to.

"Well, if you must know, I did have a thing for John. That was a long time ago though, it's all over now. Nothing really happened with us."

"What do you mean nothing *really* happened? What exactly went on with both of you? Did you sleep with him or something? Jesus Karen, I knew you liked him more than just as a friend – I can see it in your eyes when you look at him." Steven had never been a trusting person, especially of his girlfriends. "Come on Karen, fess up. Tell me all about it, I want to know."

"Oh come off it Steven. First of all, I know you. You don't really want to know what happened. I know that you aren't going to believe me anyway," Karen said, adding, "But, if you must know, I kissed him. That's it. I kissed him one night back in college; he didn't even kiss me back. It was just stupid college shit, don't worry about it."

"Oh sure, I bet that's all it was. Even if he didn't kiss you back it doesn't change the way you obviously felt about him. I bet you still want him now yet. Can't I trust you with anyone? I don't want you hanging out with him anymore Karen, you got it?" Steven's voice had begun to raise, in sync with his blood pressure.

"No, I don't 'got it' Steven. I've been friends with John and Shawna for far longer than I've known you," Karen said, disgusted with the way Steven was treating her. "If anyone is going to be subtracted from this equation it's going to be you. If you don't want to hang out with John anymore then do that, but don't expect me to drop my friends at your whim. Now, have you 'got it' Steven?"

"Whatever. I don't even want to talk about it anymore. Just thinking about you with that asshole makes me feel sick."

"Asshole? Five minutes ago he was one of your best friends, Steven. I'm going to let you figure this one out on your own. If you are going to break of your relationship with him over something I did like three years ago, you go right ahead. You're the asshole here Steven," Karen said, slamming the door behind her as she left Steven's apartment.

From that night on Steven refused to go out with John and Shawna and became infuriated with Karen each time she did. Karen's relationship with John and Shawna weakened due to Steven's behavior, but the three remained friends. Karen was Shawna's maid of honor for their wedding, and was there for John to support him after Shawna passed away while giving birth to Dakota. All this time Steven refused to make amends, and it was for this same reason that he was infuriated at the thought of John escorting Karen, *his* girlfriend, to the AHDATA gala.

"Fucking asshole..." John muttered under his breath. "Bastard better keep his hands to himself, I'll say that much." John reached to the handle and opened his car door, letting the brisk air fill the vehicle. He shut his eyes for a minute and got out of the car. "And now I have to deal with this shit. I hope to God no one here tries talking to me," he thought. "Where the hell is Miles when you need him?"

At that moment Steven saw Miles's car turn the corner into the alleyway. Steven hurried over to the car, rapped on the passenger-side window, and motioned for Miles to open the door. Miles opened the door and Steven climbed into the passenger seat.

'You see this shit man? It's crazy – I figured there'd be some people down here but never this much. What, did they get word Detective Kevin Miles was coming down? I bet that's it. We all know how damned popular you are."

Fifteen[5]

"Jesus, it smells like something died in here," said Steven. "Would you mind getting that light out of my face? I can't see a thing."

Miles handed a flashlight to Steven who then swept it throughout the empty wooden shell of the abandoned brewery. Bits of dust floated through the beams of light, gently illuminating like the ghosts of fireflies as they gracefully passed. The floor was made of the same wooden slat boards as the walls, and a few boards were missing in places, opening up to small pits of dirt below. The brewery had been built in the early 1900s and abandoned since the taxes of Prohibition force it to cease operation. Almost all of the original equipment had been removed, either sold, junked, or stolen. As Steven ran his flashlight across the void beyond, he could make out nothing in the emptiness other than a half-dozen wooden brewing barrels in the corner closest to him.

Their flashlights offered the only light; all the windows had been knocked out over the years from vandals and had been boarded up by the city to keep people from entering the building. It was a health risk, a law-suit waiting to happen. In fact, it had been scheduled to be torn down several times since its condemnation, but the Courtsdale Historical Soci-

[5] Play Audio: "Eyes Without a Face" by Billy Idol

ety saved the building of such a horrible fate. It was a historical landmark, they said. One of our few reminders of what old Courtsdale was like.

It was also be a great place to strip a priest naked, cut his eyes out, and hang his lifeless body like an art-deco tapestry.

“Is that better?" asked Miles. “Can you see now?”

“Yeah, that’s better.” Steven coughed lightly, clearing the dust that had begun to settle in his throat. “My God, what *is* that smell? You smell that Miles? It smells like rancid bacon or something. Did you forget to brush your teeth after lunch or what?” Steven’s joking was an exterior fashion only. We wore his hubris lightly, attempting to avoid the feeling of panic that could wash over him at any moment. He tended to have an overactive imagination and simply being here, in the dark empty carapace of an abandoned brewery, with the smell of a rotten *something* filling the air lent itself to wild speculation.

He could imagine it. In the distance, just beyond the reach of his flashlight – behind the dusty stack of barrels perhaps – there was surely someone lurking. A wild-eyed psycho hunkered down in the corner, naked but for a pair of oily dirt-stained briefs, playing marbles with his recently acquired eyes as shooters. Actually no, the person was probably a regular-looking Joe – Eugene maybe. Killers were usually the most normal of people; they just have a few screws loose. And he was probably moving closer. Skulking in the shadows, shimmying along the rafters, knocking dust down from above to flutter about in Steven and Miles’ flashlights. He could feel the killer’s breath on the back of his neck. Warm. Soft. Sticky.

"What the *fuck* is that smell!" Steven yelled nervously. "Damn it Miles, what are we doing in here anyway?" He had taken about as much imagination as he could handle. Something about the place, about the dark, dry, foul-smelling place left him uncomfortable.

"Would you calm down Steven? The only reason we came in here is so that I could talk to you without having to deal with the crowd outside. We already combed every inch of this place yesterday. You saw the tape on the door. It's considered a crime scene, reporters aren't allowed in here. They stay out there while we're in here. Get it? No interruptions from the masses. You should be grateful I even let you in here. I'm granting you a privilege."

"Couldn't you have talked to me someplace else maybe? Someplace that didn't smell like the dead cat I found at my grandmother's farm when I was eleven? This place is creepy as hell."

"Sure, I could have talked to you somewhere else. But then I wouldn't have been able to show you this."

Intrigued by what Miles could be referring to, Steven suddenly forgot about his imaginary predator looming in the rafters above. He forgot about the dark and he forgot about the smell. He simply turned his flashlight to Miles and asked, "What do you have to show me?"

"Oh man, you are going to love this. It's back there, behind the barrels. Come with me, I'll show you."

As they walked across the barren floor, boards creaking below their feet, Steven's imagination started back up. Behind the barrels, he knew, would be the body of a wild-eyed crazy man, dressed only in dirt and oil-stained briefs. His dead hand clutching the eye of Father Bergens, the other eye gone – eaten probably. What they found was not nearly as gruesome, but it made Steven gag reflexively nonetheless.

There on the floor with bits of dust clinging to the edges was a pair of eyes.

"Funny thing is, they weren't here when we checked the place out last night. Whoever the killer is, he must have come back sometime last night and put them here. We don't know how he got in, the tape looked undisturbed, but then again he could have come in another way. This place is nothing but a bunch of loose boards; he could have easily pried one of these off and come in that way. Regardless, it doesn't matter how he got in, just that he got in. And he put these here."

"Didn't you have someone here watching the building overnight? I mean, you'd think your buddies down at Policeman Land would have had the brains to put someone on the building to watch for suspicious activity or something."

Miles ignored Steven's condescending attitude, chalking it up to a case of dark-place jitters. "Well when you got down here we had already checked the entire place out. All we had left to do was get the body down and to the morgue. You didn't think I'd call you down right in the middle of an investigation did you? We have to be able to get some things done without you fucking it all up, right?" Miles smiled, noticed Steven's stern, inquisitive face, and continued, "Anyway, all our investigation stuff was done. Why would the killer come back here? The murder happened a few days ago. He knew the body was gone and everything had been cleaned. If he had left anything behind we would surely have found it. So we just taped it off in case we needed to check anything else out."

"Okay, but how did you know they were here now? Who found them? Why are these eyes still rotting on the dirty floor? Shouldn't they be picked up and examined or something?"

"Well that's why I was coming down here. We've had officers stationed down here since your story ran. There have been hoards of people coming to check out where the murder took place, mostly media and sick bastards who get a kick out of things like this. Well some A-hole decided it would be cool to cut through the tape and go looking around in here. Luckily Deputy Rankin saw and intervened before he could cause any serious damage. The guy had just cut the tape and gotten into the building when Rankin stopped him – didn't get a chance to see anything."

"Wait, you said the tape was undisturbed. Some dude cut it? How do you know the elusive eye-bandit didn't come in through the door?"

"Well, it was undisturbed except for that," Miles answered sheepishly. "Besides, that's not what's important. What's important is that the eyes are here. Rankin found them when he did a once-through of the premises."

"So how do you know the tape-cutter wasn't the one who put the eyes here?" asked Steven. "Maybe he was your murderer and you let him get away."

"No, it wasn't him. We aren't that stupid, Steven. The tape cutter was some new reporter over at Channel Seven. I forget his name."

Steven nodded. "Typical."

"So, about the eyes… I was hoping you could help me with something. Since you're the biggest "expert" I know." Miles lowered his body closer to the eyes, kneeling in the thin dust on the floor below. "Does this look like it was some sort of cult or satanic killing thing? I mean, I know that's all bullshit, but the people who believe in that stuff are big believers. And I know they believe in killing and doing stuff like this. You know, human sacrifice and all that jazz."

"What, do you mean how the guy cut out the eyes? Or how he was hung on the wall?"

Miles moved closer to Steven, looking over his shoulder to make sure they were alone in the darkness. "Well, mostly the eye thing," he whispered. "Whoever killed Father Bergens obviously didn't cut the eyes out by accident. And it was no accident that they just "magically" appeared back here on the brewery floor."

Steven paused for a minute, contemplating the possibility. "Take a look at the eyes, Miles. Do you see how they are arranged?"

Miles returned his gaze to the two lifeless eyes below. They had begun to dry out, but only recently. They had obviously been taken care of in the time between the killing and now. Still, Miles noticed nothing in particular about their placement on the floor. He wasn't sure what he was missing. He nodded his head "no," keeping his eyes on the eyes on the floor.

"That's right, there isn't anything particular about how they are placed - and that's the thing. The killer, well, he just," Steven held his hand in a fist over the two shrunken, rotting eyes, then opened his fist – palm hovering above the floor. "He just 'plop' – dropped them on the floor. You can even see a bit of splatter from when they hit, there in the dust. Notice how the dust film is a little off-colored in a kind of halo around the eyes? They were probably still wet when he dropped them. This means that the guy, or girl if you want, wasn't doing it for some sort of cult or voodoo thing or any crap like that. What it does mean, however, is that he didn't give a shit about the eyes. He cut them out because he thought it would look cool if he cut them out. He did it for the reaction. He didn't care one bit about them. The only reason you ever even saw them again was because he wants to fuck with you. He's laughing at you from the shadows."

"Damn," was all Miles could reply. The two sat there for what seemed like an eternity until Miles slowly stood back up, slowly brushing the dust from his knees.

"What do you say we get out of here?" asked Miles. "I can get a forensics team in here to take care of this. I think I've had about all I can handle right now."

"Barry's?" asked Steven.

"Barry's," Miles replied.

Sixteen

The clock was nearing the two o' clock hour by the time Miles and Steven finally made it to Barry's Diner. The normal lunch-time crowd had dwindled; the only customers in the restaurant were a couple in the corner booth and a few meaty construction workers seated at the dining bar. The radio was off, and the air filled with only the random chatter of voices and the occasional clang of pots and pans from the kitchen area. Steven scanned the diner; Debbie was nowhere to be seen.

"Looks like Debbie must have the day off today," Steven said.

"Heh," chuckled Miles. "Figures you'd be the one to notice that."

"Oh, whatever. I'm just saying she's not here. It's not like I'm going to cry or anything."

The two seated themselves at their usual booth near the window, not even bothering to pick up a menu as they sat down.

"They've got chicken dumplings today. It's Wednesday – dumpling day."

Miles nodded to Steven as a waiter approached them. He must have been new; neither Steven nor Miles had seen him in the diner before.

"Hello," said the waiter. "Can I get you guys anything to drink? Coffee maybe?" His voice was jittery, stumbling over the words. In his left hand he was clicking a pen nervously.

"Listen," Steven looked at the young man's nametag, "Phil. I'm not going to have anything to eat today, but if you could be a good man and get me a cup of coffee it would be much appreciated."

"I already know what I'll be having," said Miles. "So, if you could just take the order now I'd appreciate it."

The waiter looked to Miles, to Steven, then back to the kitchen area. His look was that of confusion, like it was beyond comprehension to order food before a drink. Poor Phil was obviously confused.

"Phil. Phil!" Miles roared. "All I want is a bowl of the chicken dumplings; that, and a glass of water. I'm pretty sure you can handle that, can't you?"

Phil the waiter's face turned white at the sound of Miles's raised voice. Still he diligently wrote the order down in a little notepad pulled from his pocket and retreated back to the kitchen, mission sternly in mind.

"Maaaan," groaned Steven, rolling his eyes toward the kitchen area. "I just don't get it."

"What don't you get? It's obviously his first day, he's just learning. Cut him some slack, will you?"

"Huh? What are you talking about?" questioned Steven. "Oh, the kid. I'm not talking about him. What I don't get is how you are always hungry. I can't even think about eating right now. Brrrr!" Steven shivered at the memories of their discovery in the darkened brewery. Right now some poor forensics folk were busy cataloging and referencing the scene; recreating it in paper so diligently as to not miss a detail. Once input in the computer the act would be forever immortalized. Talk about divine acts.

"Oh, well I don't know. I just wasn't really thinking about it I guess. Plus I'm really hungry. All I ate for breakfast today was a bagel I left in my locker from yesterday. It wasn't very fulfilling, trust me."

"Here you guys go," said Phil the waiter as he placed a bowl of soup in front of Miles and filled Steven's cup with coffee. "Let me know if you need anything else, I'll be around."

"Ahem," Miles grunted. "The crackers?"

"Got you covered," Phil beamed as his right hand dove into his apron pocket, fishing out two double-packs of some generic-brand of soda cracker. After placing them on the table he remained standing there, at the table smiling blindly at Miles and Steven, obviously tickled by his own preparedness.

"Uh… yeah." Steven said flatly. He paused for a second then continued, "So… can you go away now?"

Miles spooned his soup diligently, as if inspecting the contents for possible contamination. An empty gaze of introspection enveloped his face as his right hand gently stirred the soup and he crumbled his crackers into the bowl with his left. He was obviously contemplating something. His eyes glazed as he stared deep into the bowl, searching the shallow pool of broth oceans and cracker islands before him for some profound discovery Miles too would discover, if he just looked carefully enough.

"Do you ever think about stuff Steven?" asked Miles, his gaze not straying from the stirring of his soup.

"Well… I suppose that depends on what you mean by 'stuff', Miles. I think about things, yeah."

"I guess what I mean is… ummm…" Steven hesitated. "Do you ever think about *important* things? I mean things that we don't normally think about – deeper stuff."

"What? Like the meaning of life? I guess I've thought about it a few times, it doesn't occupy my thoughts that often though."

"I guess stuff like that, but other things too. Like take right now for example, do you ever think about right now – where we are, when we are, what we're doing?"

"You mean, is there a meaning behind what we do, right? I'd like to think there is, otherwise why else would we be doing it?"

"No, that's not what I'm talking about. Let's see…" Miles paused, looking up toward Steven. "Here we are, sitting in this diner – in Barry's diner. We're in this certain booth, the one we call "our" booth. But it isn't really ours, is it?"

Steven looked quizzically at Miles, and was just about to respond when Miles continued, "There are hundreds, maybe thousands, of other people who've sat here, in "our" booth. Just think of all the stories this booth could tell. All kinds of secrets have probably been shared here. Love has probably both blossomed and died here, moments have been shared, and it's all part of this place. We're part of this place, Steven – just like the people who sat here before we came in. This place has stories Steven; every place has stories. Just imagine if places could talk."

"Okay… I'm not sure what you're getting at, but I'm still listening."

"Places have stories, as do people. Think of all the hearts and souls we've each touched in our lives. It's pretty amazing when you think about it. Just think if you and I had never met, our lives would be incomprehensibly different. Every person and every place affects each other, it's a symbiotic relationship. We come here; we bear ourselves to this booth. The booth takes on part of us and we take on part of the booth, part of this place. It becomes part of our person."

"Yeah, I know what you mean," Steven replied. "I was thinking about something related to this earlier this morning, and even more so on the way here. Think about Father Bergens, so many people trusted him with their secrets. Who knows how many times he's given confession – thousands I bet. Think about the secrets he knew, but was never able to tell. Things like that must really wear a person down."

"Right, and if a person takes in so many secrets, where do they all go?" Miles responded. "If he's heard about so many bad things that people have done, do their bad things start to manifest in him?"

"I have no idea, but what I do know is this: a priest bears witness to secrets and souls and hearts, just like a booth – or any place for that matter. But the difference between the two is that a person understands the significance of a secret or a moment. This booth, it doesn't understand what we are saying; it's really only a witness. This booth cannot judge us for what we say, and it can't share our secrets with others. And in even greater contrast, unlike a priest, this booth doesn't believe it has some kind of power where it can save you by listening to your secrets, and it certainly can't say you're forgiven and magically clear them from your conscience. A priest believes his power is handed to him from on high. He believes it's his duty to listen to our secrets, then hand out forgiveness for "sins" at his own discretion: two Hail Mary's, three Our Father's

– and all is forgiven – your soul is clean! That's all it takes and the priest thinks he has power over everyone else."

"All right Steven, calm down," interjected Miles. "Sorry to interrupt your rant, but I have to go use the restroom. I'll be back in a minute."

"Fine, go ahead," Steven replied.

That's all it really takes, and these people think they can forgive us, thought Steven. *The power of God? Fools. There is no power of God, there is only the power of man and the power of man to control his fellow man. That's the real power of religion – strong people ruling the weak.* Steven paused for a second and looked out the window as the raindrops began to fall once again, refilling the nearly dried puddles from the morning rain. *Oh well, fucker's dead now anyways. Guess he learned his lesson in the end after all.*

"Steven? You about ready to get going?" Miles had returned from the bathroom and was putting his jacket on. "I've got some things to take care of yet today, so I'd like to take you back to your car so I can go get them done."

"Oh… yeah… yeah, I'm ready to go," Steven replied, turning his gaze back to the rain outside. "Hey, did you maybe want to go out for a few drinks tonight? I really need to get out of my apartment, for a reason other than work, for once."

"Yeah that's cool. Now get your jacket on so we can get out of here. It's raining like a bitch out there."[6]

---

[6]Play Audio: "I Am a Wicked Child" by Radiohead

Seventeen[7]

The corner penthouse on the 22nd story of the Brittingham Arms Apartments was one of the most highly coveted apartments in downtown Courtsdale. Beyond its double-oak doors was a polished marble entryway, which in turn opened into a grand living quarters of flecked granite and brushed steel fixtures. The walls facing the outside consisted of double-paned one-way glass. The curtains were open, and the lights of downtown Courtsdale cast a yellow glow upon the quiet apartment. John Paluniak was pacing back and forth on the phone through the foyer; Dakota was busy playing in his bedroom down the hall.

"… I'm just double-checking that you're going to be here is all. This is very important, and I have to make sure I'm there on time." He moved the phone between his ear and shoulder, freeing up his hands so he could tuck his shirt into his fitted tuxedo pants. "Yes. Yes, that's right. I'll see you then. Goodbye."

---

[7]Play Audio: "Ladies and Gentleman We Are Floating in Space" by Spiritualized

John switched the phone off, placed it in its base, and proceeded to fasten the buttons on his shirt. He reached into his pants pockets and pulled out a pair of solid gold cufflinks, then paused for a bit and gripped them in his hand as he walked to his bedroom. On the dresser was a small cream-colored china dish. Small and shallow, it was the kind of dish generally used for crushing spices. The sides were decorated with an intricate green and red floral pattern with tiny diamonds encrusted in each flower's center. John picked up the china dish and dumped its contents into the top dresser drawer. He placed the cufflinks in the dish and grabbed a pair of black opal cufflinks from inside the drawer instead.

Two years ago John dealt with the hardest part of losing Shawna. The house he and she lived in was too big for John to take care of alone, and he wasn't about to hire a maid. He and Dakota didn't need so much space, John had told himself. So when this apartment at Brittingham Arms opened up, John opted to sell the house and move back downtown.

In reality, it was the memories of Shawna that forced John to move on. Every bit of the house reminded him of her; each time he stepped through the doorway he was reminded of the first time he carried his wife over the threshold.

During the move John did one of the most difficult things he had ever been faced with – part with Shawna's things. Moving all her things to the new apartment would be questionable. People would say he couldn't let go, that he still thought she might come back one day. In his head, John knew he had to move on. So, as much as it hurt him, one day John sat down and went through the closets and boxes and drawers, sorting out Shawna's belongings. Her hairbrush that still smelt of her shampoo, the pair of shoes she only wore once because the heel broke before they had even left the house, the set of paints she bought in hopes of becoming an artist but never even opened – they all had to go.

Tears rolled down John's face as he remembered this, sorting through it all to decide what would stay and what would go. He had promised himself one box; one box of Shawna's things was all he would keep. Memories were memories, they were things that had happened and they would stay a part of him. Keeping their catalysts wasn't necessary, just because the things were sent away didn't mean the memories were.

The dish on the dresser had been Shawna's, one of the few things John had decided to keep. The gold cufflinks were a gift from her father, a gift for their wedding. John had kept those too; they were his best. Tonight, however, was not the proper occasion to be wearing them, especially since he would be attending the dinner with another woman. It didn't matter that the woman was Karen – he knew Shawna would have understood but John himself could not.

"Dakota," John shouted over his shoulder, wiping a tear from his eye. "Kelly's going to be here soon, I'd like it if you would put away some of your toys before she gets here."

Straightening his tie in front of the mirror, John saw Dakota emerge behind him from the dark hallway. Seeing his son always brought a smile to his face. So, smiling, John turned around to face his son. Already wearing his favorite pajamas, a pair of light blue pants bottoms and a top decorated with pictures of assorted bugs, Dakota smiled back at his father. He rubbed his eyes roughly, accustoming them to the bright lights of his father's room. In his right hand he clutched the arm of his ragged teddy bear, George. As he rubbed his eyes George flailed about wildly, dragged along for the ride from the floor to Dakota's face, and back to the floor again.

"Come here, big guy." His voice nearly choked as his heart swelled at the sight of his little boy. "Give your dad a hug." John dropped to his knee and Dakota scurried from the doorway, leaping into his father's strong arms.

"Daddy, why do you have to go?" questioned Dakota. "I want to watch Lion King."

"Well," John chuckled, "you can watch Lion King with Kelly. She'll be here soon. Aunt Karen and I are going to an important dinner tonight. Besides, you like Kelly; I even got some ice cream for you two to eat tonight while you watch it."

"Awww dad, I want to watch it with *you.*" Dakota pulled back a bit and looked up to his father with his round, wet eyes.

"How about this: you and Kelly hang out tonight, eat some ice cream, and watch Lion King. Then tomorrow night you and I will do whatever you want. How does that sound?" John hated to let his son down, and whenever he heard sadness in Dakota's voice, it tore into his heart. Still he knew he couldn't give in to Dakota's every wish, and tonight was not something he could miss.

"All right, Dad," replied Dakota. "You're going out with Karen? She seemed sad today, why is she sad?"

John had no idea why Karen would be sad unless Steven had done something again; the last time he heard from her she seemed excited at the idea of going out. Undoubtedly this was a big event for her; she and Steven rarely did anything even close to cultural together. Going to the Gala would be good for her.

"I don't know why she's sad, Dakota. I'm sure she'll be fine though. Just you see, tomorrow when you see her she'll be good as new."

"I hope so, I don't like it when she's sad."

"Neither do I son, neither do I." John's voice trailed off and he hugged his son again.

The sound of a ringing phone interrupted their hug. John let go of his son, hurried to the kitchen to answer the phone before the machine did.

"Hello?"

"Miss Cerys is here, Mr. Paluniak," a refined voice replied. The Brittingham Arms was fully staffed with doormen and a service / security desk in the lobby. Visitors were required to check in at the front desk, and would not be allowed to enter any of the suites beyond without prior authorization or direct confirmation from a resident. It was all part of the building's Enhanced Security Protocol, or ESP. The man at the other end of the line, Daniel Farmouth, was recently appointed as Security Director of ESP. In his late fifties, Daniel's previous position was desk manager. Corbin Brittingham, Daniel's brother-in-law, owned and managed Brittingham arms. Rumor had it Daniel got the position as a favor to Brittingham; a payment for not informing Mrs. Brittingham about Mr. Brittingham's various lady callers.

"Send her up," John replied. "You know she's always welcome here, Daniel."

"Right, right," said Daniel. "Go right on up, Miss Cerys." John could hear Daniel speaking to her; he hadn't covered the mouthpiece on the phone receiver. "She's on her way up now, Mr. Paluniak."

"Thank you, Daniel. Goodbye." John hung up the phone and called to Dakota, "Dakota, I told you to pick up your things from the living room. Kelly's going to be here any minute. Can you please at least put your trucks back in your toy box?"

"Yeah, yeah," said Dakota, stomping his feet emphatically on the ground as he trudged past John into the living room. With each toy he placed back in his toy box, he let out a heaving sigh, signifying the tremendous amount of work that had been requested of him. Before putting away more than four of his toys, a ring from the doorbell announced Kelly Cerys's, the babysitter's, arrival.

John walked down the dimly lit hallway towards the door. He walked slowly, both to afford Dakota a few more moments to put away his toys and to ensure he had regained his composure from the emotional breakdown only minutes earlier. He winced as a static spark jumped from his fingertips to the doorknob, briefly illuminating the entryway with a ghostly blue glow.

At seventeen, Kelly Cerys seemed a bit old to be a babysitter. She had, however, been Dakota's babysitter since just after his birth. Originally John had planned on asking Karen to watch Dakota on the nights he had to go out. He ultimately decided against it though, feeling too much time spent between Karen and Dakota may lead him to look to her as a replacement mother. John didn't want that to happen. Besides, Karen had her own life to deal with. She still spent more time with Dakota during the day than most parents ever spend with their children - John, himself, excluded. Kelly was one of those "friend of a friend" referrals, and John was a bit hesitant at first to allow his child to be taken care of by a stranger. After meeting with her, however, John decided to give her a try. Since then Kelly and Dakota developed a relationship more akin to that of sister-brother than babysitter-job.

Kelly was still in eighth grade when she first started watching Dakota. She was now a senior in high school. Over the past years John watched her grow from a geeky, freckled adolescent to a beautiful auburn-haired young woman. She had a boyfriend now, making it more difficult for John to find nights where she was open so he could go out. At the end of the year she'd be graduating from high school and going off to college somewhere. He'd have to find a new babysitter eventually, but he wasn't looking forward to it.

"Hey Kelly! How've you been?" John asked, holding the door for her as she entered the apartment.

"Oh, you know, I've been getting along," she replied, smiling He could smell a hint of chorine in her hair as she walked by; she must have come from swim practice.

"Team doing alright? What are you guys ranked now?"

"We're actually in the off-season right now," Kelly corrected him. "I was just doing some laps after school to keep in shape. Gotta stay fit, right Mr. P?" She smiled again and flipped her still damp hair back over her shoulder as she continued down the hallway.

"Oh yeah, right. Sorry about that,' said John. "Anyway, I have to get going right away. I can't be late for this thing – you know how it is. You know where everything is here, and you know all the rules. There's a pint of cookie dough ice cream in the freezer for you guys to pig out on, if you want. I promised Dakota he could have some. Make sure he doesn't eat too much though; you know how he gets."

"I know, I know. Everything will be fine, just like usual. Get going, I'll take care of it," she reassured him. "Dakota, come here and give your dad a hug and kiss goodbye," she shouted over the breakfast counter into the living room. Dakota poked his head up from behind the couch and came running. George was still in tow, his eye making a clacking sound as his face was dragged across the tile flooring.

"Bye bye daddy. You'll tuck me in when you get home, right?" Dakota asked innocently.

"Of course I will, big guy," John replied. "I'll give you a hug and a kiss again too." John grabbed his keys from the counter and turned to leave. "You two have fun tonight, I'll see you soon." He waited until he heard the door close behind him before freeing his tears. He always dreaded saying goodbye to his son.

Karen's apartment was on the West side of town, about a twenty-minute jaunt from John's. With a little bit of quick maneuvering and a generous interpretation of the speed limit, he managed to make it there in just under thirteen minutes. Karen was waiting on the front stoop of her building, enjoying a cigarette she quickly snuffed as she saw John's car pull up to the curb. Slinging the small black leather purse she reserved for special occasions over her shoulder, she hurried down the steps to the sidewalk as quickly as her heels would allow her to.

John, ever the gentleman, exited the car to open the door for her. As he approached the passenger's side, he couldn't help but pause to take in the gorgeous woman before him. Karen, although by no means a tall woman, was a pure beauty of elegant skin and legs bathed in a long, tight-fitting strapless dress. Her hair was pulled back and held in place with two chop sticks; a small waft of which fell across the pale skin of her face, just past her eyes. She radiated sexiness and allure; although she could never see it herself. John simultaneously felt feelings of want and of disgust, for at this moment his body badly wanted Karen while he was disgusted by the realization she was being wasted on a man like Steven.

Without saying a word, John swiftly opened the door for Karen, standing aside as he did to allow her to enter the vehicle. Once she was seated, he closed the door, walked to the other side and reentered the car, and the two began to drive.

After nearly a minute of silence, Karen burst out laughing. "What is it with you? Are you trying to be Mr. Debonair tonight? Don't you know you have to sweet talk a lady too? You can't just expect to be suave and have that do all the work for you," she said, the words interspersed with bursts of amusement. "I'm not that easy, you know!" She laughed again and looked sternly towards John, pushing her lower lip out in a melodramatic pout.

John looked over to Karen, and couldn't help but laugh himself. "Oh yes Miss Sexy One. I know you're so far beyond my reaches I could never *hope* to get with you. I honestly feel flattered just to have you speak to me." The two joked a lot, and it was this bit of idiotic humor that had no doubt kept Karen sane all these years. She loved to joke with John; he was like her brother and she loved him as one, if not more so.

"So John, how come you were late? You're going to disappoint a lot of people if you're not at your little shindig tonight on time. It's a big deal; I've seen it plastered all over the papers. It seems like they've been talking it up a lot more this year than last."

"First of all, I was what, two minutes late? We'll be there in plenty of time. You forget you're with the master of the wheel tonight, baby!" joked John. "Anyway, the reason it's been hyped so much is because we finally switched the venue for this thing. After all those years we've been having it at the Hotel Continental down on First and Jefferson, we've found ourselves a new – more exotic locale, if you will."

"How in God's green Earth did you manage that anyway? I didn't think the museum was rent-able for events, even important events like your fundraising benefit."

"It's not," John replied. Then, after a short dramatic pause he turned to Karen and continued, "I just happen to know people who know people."

"Ooh, you sly dog you! You're a man who gets things done!"

"Yes I am … yes I am. And speaking of getting things done, I'm done driving – we're here."

The Humphrey Museum was the most elegant building in Courtsdale. Built entirely of stone and marble in the late 19th Century, it was also one of the oldest. The building was originally constructed to serve as an armory, should Courtsdale be attacked during the Civil War. After a few short years, however, it became evident the building was being wasted in its current state and was causing an unnecessary bit of uneasiness with the general population of Courtsdale, who were uncomfortable having the most prominent building in downtown at the time be shelter for such a cavalcade of weapons. Thus it was decided it could serve a better purpose as a museum, given a few renovations and expansions.

Four series of wide granite steps led to the massive marble archway. The twenty-foot tall solid wood doors were propped open, and as John and Karen entered the building Karen couldn't help but feel miniscule in comparison. She paused beneath the arches; such a big building – such a big event, and she was such a small, insignificant person. Her stomach dropped as she realized she felt wholly out of place.

"Something wrong?" asked John, after realizing she was no longer beside him. He walked back to her, and put out his elbow. She nodded "no," put her arm in his, and the two continued onward.

"Don't worry," John assured her. "You're with me, so you're totally in. Besides, you look smokin' tonight."

Karen shrugged. "I guess…" She then smiled, forcing herself to at least appear comfortably happy.

"Think of it this way: there are going to be plenty of high-rollers here tonight. You look ravishing and these guys all have a boatload of money. Maybe you can find yourself a rich man."

"Don't even start with that shit, John," Karen replied, only this time her smile was not forced. "Let's just get this night going."

Eighteen

"She had better not sleep with him. If he touches her, so help me I'll cut his nuts off and throw them in the sewer."

"Would you quit that shit already, Steven? I thought we were going out to have a *good* time tonight, not for you to sit there and stew about your girlfriend. I'm trying to drive here, and listening to you bitch doesn't help my concentration."

Steven and Miles were on Fourth Avenue on their way to The Keep, a dive bar on the outskirts of downtown. Miles had picked Steven up from his home in his Grand Am. He didn't feel safe letting Steven drive tonight, as he was fairly certain Steven was going to drink much more than what Miles felt safe with, should Steven be behind the wheel. Steven had been in a rotten mood when Miles called him earlier to see if he still wanted to go out. Miles had to think twice about even going out, until Steven assured him he'd quit the shit. Five minutes into their drive and Steven had already gone back on his word.

"Fine, fine," said Steven. "So how was home? Kids alright? How's the wife?"

"Home's good, nothing new going on there, just the same old stuff. I was only there for about an hour tonight for dinner before coming to pick you up. I didn't get out of work until almost six; we had a meeting about the whole Bergens thing."

Steven immediately perked up. "Oh really? Anything interesting happen in the meeting? I don't suppose you cracked the case already?"

"Heh, far from it my friend. We still don't know a damned thing about what happened, other than the obvious. The autopsy didn't turn up anything more than what you were there for; we're still waiting on the tox screen to come back – I'm told we might have it tomorrow. I don't expect to find anything in there anyway though."

"So what, you haven't found anything new at all? Did you get anything interesting from the interviews you guys did? I know you talked to Sister Katherine – so I assume you talked to a few other people too. They didn't have anything interesting to say?"

"Not really. He was living a normal life – no threats or anything, if that's what you mean. There weren't any enemies that anyone could come up with. Mostly the people were so shocked and saddened that it was hard to get anything coherent out of them in the first place, but once we did they didn't have much to say anyway. The best we can come up with is that it's either some sort of cult or satanic kind of deal; at the very least the person who did it more than likely has issues with either the church or organized religion in general."

"That makes sense," Steven nodded his head as he replied. "I mean, what with the fact that they killed a priest, and then crucified him. Maybe they thought he wasn't worthy to be a priest or something. Like, he was preaching something different from what the church believed. Maybe one of the parishioners did it because they thought we were guilty of blasphemy. That's what happened to Jesus, right? The major leaders of the time thought his preaching was against accepted doctrine, and they had him killed for blasphemy. If someone from the church, or someone familiar with Bergens's preaching thought he was spouting off untruths, isn't it possible that could be the motive?"

"I think you're reaching a bit, Steven," Miles replied. "Besides, we already thought of that as an option. The problem is that, at least as far as we can tell, he wasn't doing anything radical there. Everyone says he was your regular straight-and-narrow priest, never crossing the line at all. So, it's pretty doubtful that's the motive. I *am* glad to see you remember your Sunday School classes though."

"Fuck Sunday School," Steven responded, defensively. "I know way more about religion than you'd think, Miles. It's not like just because I don't go to church I *never* went to church. Besides, it's interesting stuff to know, even if it's more a myth than a history."

"Again, calm down. I was just giving you shit. Don't think I doubt your knowledge on anything, I know you don't go off spouting shit you know nothing about," said Miles. "What's your beef with Sunday school then, if you think it's good to know about religion."

As the car slowed to a stop at the corner of Fourth and Beecham the rain started again, sounding out a cacophony of pings as it hit the metal and glass of the car. The low rumble of thunder rolled in the distance. A cat darted into an alley and scurried below a dumpster for shelter. The light turned green, and in silence, but for the rain, Miles turned left onto Beecham.

"You really want to know?" asked Steven, as the car began to pick up speed. "Well, I guess you could sum it all up with this one song we had to sing. I don't remember all the words, but I do remember the main part."

Steven paused shortly, waiting for Miles to speak, then continued. "The song had a chorus that said 'Jesus loves me, this I know – for the Bible tells me so.' That's where my 'beef' comes from, Miles."

Miles looked at Steven quizzically. "Okay, good for you; you're tormented by being forced to sing songs in Sunday school. Christ Steven, you're not the only person who ever had to do that. Didn't you have to sing songs in regular school too? Or are you going to tell me you hate all education now?"

"No, that's not it at all," replied Steven. "It's the words to the song, *that* song in particular. Don't you get it? Jesus loves me, because the Bible says so? What the hell is that? I think that if you're going to have something to base your belief system on, it shouldn't be just because you read it in a book. That's the problem with religion, more specifically organized religion. They tell you that you should adhere to this certain belief system, or faith, and the main reason they give you is because it's written in a book. It doesn't leave room for you to make your own decisions; you're not allowed to think for yourself. If Jesus loves me, I want it to be for a reason – and I want to know it for a reason I came up with on my own. I want to witness him, in some form or another. I'm not saying you need to have some divine intervention in your life where Jesus appears to you or anything like that. I can respect people who have faith for a reason other than that they are told they should. If that's the only reason they believe, then they could believe anything so long as that's what they were brought up with believing. I don't believe because I don't have a reason to. I'm not so stupid to adamantly believe there is *no* God, what I believe is that I don't have a reason to believe in God at this time in my life. Anyway, I've gone off on a tangent. I think I answered your question though."

Once Steven finished talking, Miles sat quietly, digesting everything Steven had said – applying it to his own thoughts and reasons for his beliefs. Miles *had* felt a presence in his daily life, he had reasons to believe in God other than that he was told to do so. He could, however, see where Steven was coming from.

"You've got a really good point Steven. I totally agree with you that people shouldn't believe something just because they're told to believe it. Unfortunately, I don't feel like getting into a religious debate with you right now. Let's just have a good time tonight, sound good?"

A grin spread across Steven's face. But whether it was of happiness or of insanity, Miles couldn't quite determine.

"I'm all for that, my brother," Steven replied – still grinning.

The Keep looked fairly deserted; not many people, save for post-happy hour construction workers, visited the bar this early in the evening, especially on a Wednesday night. Steven and Miles normally wouldn't be out to the bars before nine or ten o' clock either, but Miles *did* have to be in to the precinct by eight the next morning. Besides, when Miles called Steven sounded like he needed to get out of the apartment as soon as humanly possible; he wouldn't stop fretting about Karen's "date."

The parking lot was empty except for Miles's Grand Am, a rusted out blue Monte Carlo and two motorcycles. Most likely at least one of these vehicles belonged to the staff; they'd have the place to themselves. This was actually the reason The Keep was their first stop for the evening. Both Steven and Miles both could use a break from the crowds for a bit, just enough to get the juice flowing again. A few drinks would no doubt help jump-start the process. Glass crunched below Miles' feet as he stepped on a piece of a broken beer bottle. The parking lot was covered in them.

"Jesus, this place has gone to hell," Steven remarked.

"This place has always been hell," Miles replied. "We just come here anyway."

Inside, the bar reeked of stale cigarette smoke and years of spilt beer. Steven always made sure not to come into direct contact with the bar after one time seeing a man struggle to free his bottle its unclean stickiness. These distractions aside, The Keep was a fairly decent bar with a welcoming ambiance. Its wood-centric design held a rustic flavor, the staff was generally polite, and blues music always sang from the jukebox.

"Tell me again why we keep coming back here," asked Miles.

"Beats me," Steven replied. "There's just something about this place that makes me feel good. It's almost like being home, but without the constant bickering."

There were only two people in the bar, the bartender and a woman who Steven could only deduce to be the bartender's girlfriend, given the body language of their conversation. Rather than disturb them, Steven and Miles decided to take up temporary residence in a booth.

"This round's on me," said Steven.

Surprised at Steven's sudden generosity, Miles stared blankly at Steven then said, "All right, I'll get next then. Why don't you grab me a bottle of Budweiser?"

Steven nodded and walked off toward the bar. As he was walking off, Miles heard the sound of a car entering the parking lot outside. As he heard the car door slam he could hear the sound of several people in the parking lot, then the sounds of two more cars pulling in. He looked to his watch; it was two minutes to eight. The place would start filling up soon.

Just get the beer so we can drink it and move on, thought Miles. *I don't want to have to break up any shit here tonight.*

Nineteen[8]

The Egyptian display at the Courtsdale Public Museum had recently been revamped to include an entirely new collection the museum recently acquired from a private collector. Still not open to the public, the AHDATA Gala was the first most guests had seen of its redesign. The entire west wing of the museum had been shut down for the past six months in preparation for its opening and no one, save for museum personnel, certain privileged intellectuals, and those involved in its construction, had been granted access to the area since. Security had been extremely tight given the priceless nature of the new pieces and it was even tighter tonight, given the status of some of the night's guests. One could only speculate as to how John Paluniak had managed to have the gala here. He *was* a social butterfly however - a master of networking – and it was assumed he had his fingers in at least a few pies around town.

Guests were ushered in through the exhibit's main entrance as tuxedo-clad security guards looked on. A metal detector had been built into the wood framing of the door with the hopes of increasing security while

[8] Play Audio: "Someone Great" by LCD Soundsystem

at the same time remaining subtle. However, the guests were still required to empty their pockets of any metal as they entered, sliding it through the small security windows on each side of the doorway. This managed to slow down entry greatly, but still the guests remained in high spirits, chatting with one another as each awaited his or her turn.

Although a guest of honor, John was also required to enter through the secure entrance per the museum's rigid precautions. Still, as he and Karen entered the crowd, the guests quickly moved aside to let them through. Once the crowd had separated the onlookers erupted in applause for John. Karen took a step away, uncomfortable with being at the center of attention. As she looked over to John, he took a small bow and with a roll of his wrist elegantly extended his hand to Karen. She quickly took his hand and the two continued on through the secure entrance. The guards nodded and both Karen and John walked on through the entryway, setting off the alarm as they did so. A guard quickly reset the alarm, silencing it and nodding for John and Karen to continue on.

"I can't believe how popular you are!" Karen exclaimed in a whisper as they took a seat at the head table. "It's amazing how much these people respect you; it's almost like this is a benefit in your honor."

"Come now, Karen," John said as he motioned for a maitre de to come fill their champagne glasses. "Tell me, how is it so amazing that people respect me? You make it sound like I'm some sort of flyboy."

"I'm sorry; that's not what I meant…" Karen's face flushed pink as she realized the mistake in her phrasing. "I just think it's crazy how everyone here knows you, and I'm probably the person here who's known you the longest of all."

"Yes, and you know the *real* me. So don't start telling those stories about when I used to get drunk back in college and spend all night getting sick in your toilet," joked John. "The last thing I need is for these people to know I'm an actual person."

John paused as their glasses were filled. He then stood up abruptly; picking up his glass as he did so. "What do you say we go schmooze the crowd for a bit? It's starting to fill up in here and I can't look too antisocial."

Karen's eyes lit up like moonbeams at the thought of gossip with the elite. This was a situation she had only dreamed of. It was like being a princess in one of the fairy tales of her childhood and John was the charming prince. The only difference, she thought to herself, was that when all was said and done she'd have to go home to the frog.

"Why I'd be delighted, sir." Karen's nose twitched as she tried to keep from smiling too greatly.

As they paraded across the floor, Karen was struck with awe as she realized her surroundings. She hadn't been to the museum for several years, not since college so far as she could remember. And from what she could recall, the museum was never much to brag about. Sure it had some impressive artifacts and was an interesting place to visit, but it never really grabbed her. What they'd done with the new Egyptian display, however, *grabbed* her.

The walls, draped in thick billowing red curtain tapestries were adorned with faux gold ornamentation, causing the room to appear as one large temple of sorts. On the floor against the walls were hundreds of shelves encased in glass where thousands of ornate bits of pottery and other artifacts were on display. In from the walls, more toward the center of the room, stood even more glass cases, many of these holding completely reassembled urns and golden statues encrusted with jewels Karen could only dream of wearing. The center area of the room was full of tables set up for the gala; but the true centerpiece was set in the very center of the room.

Here a large glass case was roped off with at least three feet of space on either side. Inside the case was a recreation of an actual tomb that had no doubt been pillaged years earlier. It appeared everything was present from the burial site, including a sarcophagus with the top removed and a fully mummified body held within. The lid of the sarcophagus, with several of its jewels missing, was laid down on the display's sand-covered floor next to its bottom. Various urns surrounded the sarcophagus; most were cracked and adorned with holes after thousands of years of existence.

One Arnold J. Peabody, Archaeologist and Philanthropist, had apparently donated this entire display – or so the display's sign read. The display was also supposedly a fairly exact recreation of the tomb from which it had been recovered. Karen couldn't help but feel a tinge of guilt for being so in awe of the display; here was someone's grave, uncaringly disturbed for the enjoyment of others and the "proliferation of intellect." Still, she conceded, it was an amazing display.

"Karen, I'd like you to meet David Jallick – mayor of Courtsdale." John's sudden speaking took Karen by surprise, the room still held most of her attention.

"Mr. Jallick, of course I know who you are," Karen said quickly, being sure not to come off as clueless. "It's a pleasure to finally meet you. I've read and heard so much about you."

"Hopefully only the good things," replied Jallick, matter-of-factly.

"Of course. I wouldn't have voted for you otherwise." Karen responded quickly. Her wits were thankfully with her tonight, she thought.

"Excellent! I'm only joking, you know," said Jallick. "Well, at least half-joking."

Unsure of how to respond, Karen looked around the room and pretended to have her interest grabbed by something in the far corner's display. "John, I'll catch up with you in a bit. There's something I have to check out."

"Of course," said John. "I'll be over in a bit."

"Well, it was nice to meet you Karen, even if it was only in passing." Jallick turned to John and continued, "I've got to get going too John – there are a lot of people who are going to have my head if I don't talk to them before this whole thing gets underway."

As Karen began to walk away she heard Jallick continue to John, "She seems like a good kid, John; nice catch." Karen couldn't help but smile.

For the next twenty minutes or so, Karen perused the exhibit. She was shy and didn't know any of the other guests; they weren't exactly in her social circle. Still, she smiled politely as she made eye contact with them. From time to time she would look across the room and see John talking with various people, all of whom looked important but she was oblivious as to who they actually were. Sometimes when she looked over she'd catch him looking back at her; he'd give a wink or a smile and continue on with his conversation. Karen was just happy to be there in the first place, she didn't need to talk to everyone. She finally returned to her spot at the table when she saw John too returning, motioning for her to come.

"Sorry I couldn't spend more time talking with you, Karen. These people, every one of them thinks he's my best friend. In all reality I don't know who half of these people are. I just pretend I remember them; that seems to take care of the problem most of the time. I hope you're having an alright time without me though."

"Don't be so full of yourself, mister," joked Karen. "I'm a big girl and can function perfectly well on my own, thank you very much. This place is amazing John, thanks for bringing me." She paused, and then continued, "So, when do we eat?"

"Funny you should ask," said John, motioning to the area behind Karen. "Here comes the food now." Turning around, Karen saw a crew of wait staff quickly bringing in the first course of the night's meal. As she looked throughout the room she was surprised to see everyone had taken their seats, and the room fell into a hushed silence.

Karen soon realized all eyes in the room had affixed themselves on John and her. She felt a bit uneasy at this revelation, and breathed a sigh of relief when John stood up to present a speech.

His right hand held a glass of champagne which he held out from his chest, toward the rest of the guests, as he began speaking.

"Ladies and gentlemen of the community and elsewhere," he began. "Many of you I know, and many of you I don't; but what I *do* know for certain is that we are all here because we share a similar dream. We dream of a world where disease and sickness are a thing of the past – a world where *every* person in it has the same rights to dream, the same chances of living a full life and seeing their dreams become realities."

Karen looked in front of John and around the room; no notes or teleprompter were to be found. John must have either memorized the speech or was making it up as he went along. She figured on the latter.

"The people who are gone from this world, and those who are systematically preparing themselves to leave it due to sickness, are undoubtedly grateful for your support tonight. Those most grateful are undoubtedly those afflicted with diseases and complications of the heart, which is truly what we are here to help cure. And while I know I can't speak for every one of these individuals, I do know one person in particular who I am *positive* appreciates your generosity. Shawna Paluniak, my wife, would be honored to join you tonight. She believed in putting up the good fight, in doing what we all know in our hearts to be the right thing - just as all of you do."

Karen looked deep into John's eyes as he spoke of his departed wife. She looked deep to discover tears welling up inside, but found none. Instead what she found was a glimmer of hope – a glimmer of truth in the words he was speaking. John believed every word he spoke, rather than only saying what they wanted to hear. His words were from his heart.

"Some of you may be wondering why we chose this newly redesigned – and amazing, I might add – Egyptian display as the venue for this year's AHDATA gala. And while I'm sure many of you were delighted at the thought of getting an advance look at the museum's new wing, it was more than just a clever ploy to get you to come." John smiled and paused briefly while a few chuckles rumbled through the audience.

"The ancient Egyptians took great care in preparing the bodies of their deceased for their journey to the afterlife. The first step of mummification required removing the deceased's liver, lungs, intestines and stomach and placing them in urns, which would later be placed with the body in its tomb. The brain was also removed, only to be thrown away. But the heart, on the other hand, was left in the body. You see, these people believed the heart to be the center of a person's personality; it was their link between this world and the next. The Egyptians even went so far as to include a scarab with a spell from the Book of the Dead within the body, near the heart, to assure the dead would get their heart back in the afterlife. This would assure the dead the memory of their earthly existence in the afterlife. After soaking the bodies for *40 days* in a solution of natron and wrapping the body with over 1000 yards of fine linen, a process which took another fifteen days, the heart was the only major organ to be fully preserved. You see, the ancient Egyptians, like all of us here tonight, knew that truth lie in the heart – not in the brain as we've all been taught. It's the heart which makes us strong, which stores our soul… and it's worth preserving."

John paused again to give the audience a chance to digest what he'd said, then continued, "And now that I've done my job to ruin your appetites, it's time to eat! You're going to love what we've got in store for you tonight. The servers should be bringing out your first course now, a simply delightful consommé with chervil and tomato, followed by stuffed tomato, mushroom and zucchini. There's much more to follow that, but I'll let you be surprised. Rest assured, you're going to love it."

"God John, that was a beautiful speech," said Karen as John seated himself at the table. The room was filled with applause, so Karen was forced to raise her voice. John had returned to his seat immediately after speaking. He didn't want any applause for what he had said; he'd only said what he felt necessary.

"Thanks Karen, but all I did was put what each one of us is thinking into words," he replied. "The people who really deserve the applause are everyone who came out tonight. I only wish Shawna could see all of this"

"Oh John, don't say that. You and I both know that she *is* here, and I'm sure she loves you more than ever for what you've done in her memory. There is one thing I have to know though, and be totally honest with me."

"No problem, ask away."

"How much are people paying to be here?" she asked. I mean, how much are you charging per plate, or however this thing works."

"Well, I'll tell you one thing first. If you were here as an actual date there wouldn't be a chance in hell that I'd tell you how much your plate cost. You'd think I was expecting sex later tonight," he joked.

"Well, you're not getting any," she replied, smiling. "So you can answer my question."

"Well, if you *must* know, we're charging $3000 a plate. Like I said, this is the crème de la crème of the community. We don't fuck around here, baby girl. This is the real deal."

Karen could see John's pride in the gala and all he'd done for the AHDATA as he said this, but she couldn't help but be taken aback at $3000 price point.

"Jesus, I hope you didn't have to pay for mine! I mean, shit John, you know I never would have accepted if you'd told me this before we came."

"I know," he replied. "Now eat your soup before it gets cold… and don't you dare ask for seconds."

Day Three

BEYOND CONTROL[9]

[9]Play Audio: "Not Even Jail" by Interpol

the trouble with being god

Twenty

As the woman laid out before him writhed in agony, he couldn't help but smile. The floor below was drenched in the blood spilt from her body, and after a final violent spasm she fell lifeless. The air was silent, but for the gentle "drip, drip" as the woman's blood seeped its way through the floor drain. Steven closed his eyes briefly to give his ears full sensual control but was forced to open them as a loud knocking sound jarred him back to the room.

Rather than panic, he slowly moved his eyes about the room – first to the dead girl on the floor. Her body remained lifeless and was just as he had left it when he closed his eyes. The rapping sound continued. His mind still in a fog, Steven slowly realized the sound was coming from his left.

"Steven. Steven – what are you doing?"

The voice sounded muffled, yet urgent and familiar.

"Steven – Steven!" it yelled.

Steven recognized the voice. He slowly turned his head to the source of the sound and was met by a vision of Miles. A glass wall, which Steven hadn't noticed before, was between Miles and himself. Miles rapped his fist on the glass again and spoke.

"Steve – are you alright? Wake up dammit!"

The room suddenly filled with a burst of light, and Steven opened his eyes. To his left was Miles, pounding his fist on the driver's side window of Steven's car.

"Huh? What?" Steven blinked; slowly realizing he'd been sleeping. "Oh shit, I'm up. Hold on Miles." Steven motioned with his index finger *one second*, stretched briefly, and got out of his car.

"Jesus Steven, did you sleep in your car all night long? How the hell did you end up out here anyway? When I dropped you off I had to practically *carry* you to your damn apartment; you were passed out cold before I even got out the door."

"Fuck man, would you hold on for one damned second?" Steven replied. "I just woke up, in case you forgot." He felt his brain pounding against his skull and reached up to massage his temples. "Alright," he continued, " I don't know how I got in the car actually. I don't think I went anywhere at least; the car's still parked where I left it yesterday afternoon."

"Man, that's not cool at all Steven. I hope to God you didn't go out in the state you were in last night – you could have killed someone."

"Yes, yes mother, I know. Why are you here anyway? I'm not used to getting morning wakeup calls from you – I didn't know you cared so much."

"Oh yeah, I almost forgot about that – you gotta go get yourself dressed Steven. Some serious shit went down last night; you have to see this. Oh, and take some Pepto-Bismol, there's no way your stomach is going to be able to handle what I've got to show you."

"Damn Miles, I smell like shit. Can I take a shower quick before we go, or is this another one of your 'this can't wait' scenarios?"

"No shower; just go upstairs and change. If you're not back in five minutes I'm leaving without you."

Five minutes later, Steven emerged from the front door of his apartment complex. Miles started the engine on his police cruiser and Steven seated himself in the car's passenger seat.

"Damn you smell," said Miles.

Steven lifted his arm, sniffed his armpit, and shrugged. "I told you I needed a shower, but you said no. So don't start bitching about if I smell bad or not. Where are we going, by the way?"

"Ah, that my friend, is a surprise," Miles replied. "Here, put some of this on." Miles reached for the glove compartment and pulled out a small bottle, handing it to Steven.

Steven squinted his eyes as he read the label. "Eau de Miles: sure to drive any woman insane."

"Will you quit being a jackass? Either put it on or don't. If you want everyone to start referring to you as Smelly Steven, be my guest."

"Fine, I'll put it on. Man Miles, lighten up a bit. What crawled up your ass this morning?"

"John Paluniak's mutilated body. *That's* what crawled up my ass this morning."

Twenty-One[10]

Fallen leaves spattered the surface of the Carten river below John Paluniak's office. The storms from late last night had subsided before dawn, yet the carnage of the winds and rain remained as the storm's visual evidence. Several broken branches dotted the shoreline of the river. Most trees, showing a healthy cornucopia of color only days earlier were now bare, the winds of the storm having stripped them of their autumnal beauty. Still, with sun's bright rays and perfectly clear skies the day looked warm and inviting. As always, looks could be deceiving.

Lieutenant John Pickerson turned his head from the window and back to the scene in Paluniak's office. The room was empty except for a few police officers, the coroner, and John Paluniak's desecrated body. At least that's what the dead man's ID said. Judging by the face, they couldn't be perfectly sure.

"Jesus fucking Christ…" Pickerson muttered.

Pickerson cocked his head to the side as he heard voices from the hallway. Across the room two men were ducking under the line of police tape protecting the office from the rest of the building and its inhabitants.

---

[10]Play Audio: "Posed to Death" by The Faint

The first man he recognized as Detective Miles. The second, a scruffy-looking man in disheveled clothing who had apparently not shaven or showered in at least a day or two he didn't recognize. He immediately made his way to the door to intervene.

"Detective Miles, come here this second," Pickerson ordered. "You, you stop right there and wait in the hallway," he continued, directing his voice to the other man. "You don't have clearance to be in here."

The second man slowly looked up, realizing he was being addressed. He locked eyes with Pickerson, and Pickerson could sense contempt. He then looked to Miles.

"Go wait in the hall for a second Steven. Let me talk to him; I don't know what's going on here. I told him I was bringing you in."

Steven remained stopped, half-ducked below the yellow police tape and returned his gaze to Pickerson. Pickerson looked sternly to Steven, not speaking. Steven puckered his lips and kissed the air at Pickerson snidely, then retreated back to the hallway.

"What the hell is going on here?" asked Miles. "I told you I was going to go pick up Steven Carvelle. He's been covering the Bergens case in *The Courier* and, so far as I can tell, this Paluniak murder is sure as shit connected to Bergens. Either that or we've got a whole crew of sick fucks running around this city. As messed up as this is, I'd prefer the prior. Besides," he continued, lowering his voice, "you and I both know that we're better off having Carvelle cover these stories than some sort of 'I'm working my way up the ladder' journalistic jackass. He's got a good thing going with the bureau on these cases. We know he's not going to go overboard and all melodramatic to try to turn each story into some huge overblown piece just to further his career. Having Carvelle cover these stories is the best idea anyone in the bureau has had in a long time, and I'm not about to blow this thing into a media frenzy. So, like it or not Pickerson, you're going to have to suck it up and give him privileged access to this scene."

"Alright Miles, take a deep breath and calm down. He's more than welcome in here. We both know the protocol on the press, and Carvelle's got access. Just don't let him know this, okay? So long as we keep him thinking he's lucky to get what he has, we still have the advantage. Besides, I didn't even recognize him; he looks like shit."

"Oh, yeah," said Miles. "You're right about that. I found him sleeping in his car in the parking lot at his apartment complex this morning. Not sure what happened there, he must have gone down there for some reason or another after he and I went out for a few drinks last night."

Pickerson frowned disapprovingly.

"Alright, I'll go get him and run through the scene. Hopefully he can handle it… I'll come talk to you later to get caught up on anything new."

"All right, that sounds good. But Miles…"

"Yes?"

"Don't expect me to tell you any new details when you come talk to me later."

"Why's that," asked Miles. "You can't just sit there and withhold evidence from a fellow officer because you're in a pissy mood, you know."

"It's not that," Pickerson replied. "It's just that we haven't found shit here; just what you saw when you were in this morning. I really hate cases like this."

"Ah," nodded Miles, turning back to the door to get Steven."

"Hold on a second Miles, I'm not done yet."

Miles stopped with his back to Pickerson and turned his head so he could see him. "What else do you want?" Miles didn't hide his feelings of annoyance at inconveniences of Pickerson's discussions.

"Stop thinking so much of yourself, Detective. Not everything that goes on here revolves around you. You'd do good to learn that. Each one of us has a job to do," he said. "Now go do yours and escort little Mr. Newspaper through the room, and make it quick. I don't want to deal with any more nuisance than necessary."

Miles nodded his head to the officer standing guard at the door, motioning for him to allow Steven to enter the room. The officer hesitated, looked to Pickerson who nodded in agreement, then reluctantly leaned his head out into the hallway, ushering Steven into the room. As he entered, Miles noticed a triumphant, if not brash, air to Steven's stride. He bumped the shoulder of the guard officer purposefully as he entered the room and slowly swaggered his way to Miles.

"What'd he want?" he asked. "To keep my ass out of here, I suppose." Steven answered his own question.

"Will you calm down a little Steven? We're trying to conduct an investigation here, and it would help streamline matters if you'd cooperate and not go flying off the handle right away." Miles replied. "He wasn't trying to keep you out; he just didn't recognize you in your unkempt state – and frankly, I don't blame him. Once he realized who you were he was actually happy you were here," Miles lied.

"Yeah, I'm sure," Steven replied defiantly. "So anyway, what do we have here? What's the "411," as you like to call it?"

As Steven spoke, he slowly looked around the office. Nestled on the far side of the room near the window was a large oak desk. A credenza was set out in front with several black leather office chairs arranged around it. The large chair behind the desk was pushed neatly into its place behind the desk. Behind the chair, however, several officers were gathered as well as a forensics crew. He could see one member of the group arduously taking snapshots of something on the floor behind the desk. This, undoubtedly, was where John Paluniak's body lay.

"Is that it?" asked Steven. Miles nodded his head quietly in response. "Can I take a look?"

"Go ahead, but it's not a pretty sight – to say the least."

As Steven slowly walked to the back of the room, Miles followed only as far as the credenza. Steven looked to Miles, questioning if he was coming, and Miles held up his hand to motion for Steven to go continue on his own. And so, Steven continued around to the back of the desk. As his eyes focused on the scene before him, he felt his stomach lurch. He reached for the wastebasket on the floor next to him, but only gagged. He did notice, however, the wastebasket already contained a healthy dose of vomit, most likely compliments of one of the undoubtedly green officers first on the scene.

John Paluniak's body was propped in a kneeling position facing the window overlooking the Carten River. His hands were both placed palms-up before him on the seat of a small office chair; in much the same manner Catholics hold out their hands to receive communion. Placed within the cups of his hands was a bloody mass, which through his minimal education of anatomy Steven deduced to be the man's heart. The seat of the chair was soaked in blood, as were the forearms of his white shirt. The carpet on the floor below was stained as well, from the substantial blood loss that had occurred.

Steven's eyes moved upward to the dead man's chest. Where the heart would normally be, Steven saw a large red spot of blood staining the shirt. Whoever had done this to Paluniak had either removed the heart with the man's shirt still on, or had taken the time to redress the man after he had completed his deed.

Continuing their upward journey, Steven's eyes finally met John's face. Steven hadn't seen John in years, although his girlfriend was a close friend with the man. After their bout of differences, Steven had refused to associate with him and had only seen him once or twice as he dropped Karen off from their "dates." Still, he couldn't recall the last time he had seen the man and now had trouble recognizing the face before him as someone he had once spent countless hours with – first as friends and ultimately as enemies. Now, as Steven stared deep into the holes where John's eyes should have been, he felt an impeding sensation of remorse flush through his body. He closed his eyes and turned away quickly, opening them to see Miles standing beside him.

"What…" Steven sputtered. "What in God's name happened here, Miles?"

"Like I told you, brother, John Paluniak's desecrated body is what crawled up my ass this morning. I take it you now understand my lack of joyfulness earlier," said Miles. "Let's get out of the way here and then we can talk."

Steven nodded in agreement and the two men solemnly returned to their original post in the room, allowing the other officers to continue their work. The only sound to come from the area behind the desk was the snap of the camera as it took pictures and the high-pitched whine of the flash as it recharged. Not one of the officers said a word, working in silence.

"So what happened Miles?" Steven asked, nearing hysterics. "What the *fuck* happened in here?"

"Well, best we can figure so far is that Paluniak came here late last night after the big AHDATA Gala downtown – not sure why though. Most likely he had to check up on some business or something; we're working on that. Anyway, it looks like someone must have been waiting here for him – they must have known he was coming in. The murderer, whoever he is, then killed him by cutting out his heart and eyes, then propped him in to the position you just saw him in. He's a sick bastard, whoever did this. Did you notice he took the time to button Paluniak's shirt back up over the chest wound?"

"Yeah I saw that… How do you know it's a he? Did you find some evidence to support this?"

"No, no evidence at all – but this is starting to look like the work of a serial killer. This murder is surely somehow connected to the Bergens murder, what with the eyes and all. And, since serial killers are almost always men, we're referring to the killer as "he." Besides, it's a lot easier to say than "he or she" every time."

"Sounds like a familiar argument," Steven replied. "So, why is there so little blood? I mean, I know there's a lot of blood over there, but there's no way that's all the blood that would have come out of wounds like that. He surely bled to death, and that means much more blood loss than I saw. Where'd the killer actually do the deed?"

"Good observation, Steven. While searching the

large sheet of butcher paper crumpled up and shoved into a filing cabi-net. Whoever this guy is, he was courteous enough to put papers down on the desk before he cut him up," explained Miles. "And before you ask, we're guessing he was cut up on the desk based on preliminary blood-spatter results from forensics. Blood squirted all over when the arteries were cut, and the spray pattern shows the central source to be the desk."

Steven looked back towards the desk, this time noticing the stains of blood that spotted the carpet surrounding the desk. In his head he could see John struggling as some demented surgeon cut his chest open.

"Sick," was all Steven could muster in response.

"There's more…" Miles continued. "The guy who did this, after he took care of his business, took his time replacing all the items on John's desk. We brought his secretary in here and she said as far as she could tell everything was returned to where John normally kept it."

"Jesus…" Steven replied. He looked to the desk. Everything on the desk appeared to be in its proper position, all right. Even more so, the items did not appear to be placed in a neat and orderly fashion, but rather in the positions where one would expect to find them on a desk that experienced heavy usage.

"Oh yeah, in case you didn't notice when you looked at him, John's head is looking upward, out into what would have been the night sky. The person who killed him, or his accomplice, if he has one, kept the head from falling downward by stitching fishing line on each side of the back of the victim's neck, then affixing each end to the top of its adjacent shoulder. This worked to prop the head upward without it falling down or to either side."

Steven cringed at the thought of this and found himself thanking God that he hadn't seen this for himself. What he had seen was more than enough for his liking, thank you very much.

"If I didn't know better, the way the victim was positioned you'd think he was offering his heart up to the heavens outside…." Miles trailed off into thoughts of his own. Steven preferred not to think about it at all.

"Detective Miles, could you come here? I'd like to speak to you." It was Pickerson again.

"I'll be back in a few minutes, hopefully this won't take too long," Miles said to Steven. "Stay here and don't touch anything."

Steven pretended to look around the room while Miles and Pickerson spoke. His focus kept returning to the two officers, however. He was interested to know what they were talking about. Once every twenty seconds or so Pickerson or Miles would look over, directly to Steven. Soon he got the sinking feeling his welcome had worn out. After about five minutes Miles walked back over to Steven.

"Steven, I'm going to have to ask you to – "

"It's fine Miles; I'm going. Let me know what else you find out," said Steven. "I guess I'm lucky Pickerson let me here as long as he did."

"No Steven, that's not it," Miles replied. "I'm going to – "

"Don't worry about it Miles," Steven interrupted. "I know my own way out. I'll talk to you later."

"No Steven," Miles spoke sternly this time. "I said that's not it. I'm going to have to take you in to the station for some questioning."

“You what? You’ve got to be kidding me!” Steven was beginning to shout.

“Damn it Steven. Don’t make this any more difficult than it already is. Just come with me now or I’m going to have to place you under arrest.”

Steven’s face crumpled up in incredulity. He was about to interject, then realized resistance was an exercise in futility. As he lowered his head he felt the cold metal of Pickerson’s handcuffs snapping closed on his wrists.

Twenty-Two[11]

Dusty beams of light, broken by the half-closed blinds slowly crept across the bed where Karen lay sleeping. Deep in her dream world, the face on her living body embraced a contented smile.

Karen saw herself in a green backyard beneath the rays of glorious sun shower. Ahead of her she saw John and Dakota wrestling about in the grass. In her dream she smiled lovingly at the two of them. Everything seemed to be moving in perfect slow motion, as if time in this dream life was of little consequence. *So this is what it's like*, she thought in her dream.

Suddenly Karen was distracted within her dream by a noise from behind her. She turned her focus to what seemed to be the source, only to see an image of Steven slowly coming up from behind the yard's picket fence. In his hands was a rifle. Time slowed even more, nearly stopping, and Karen felt herself scream. In her dream, Steven raised his rifle, directed it at John and fired a shot.

At the sound of her dream's gunshot, Karen woke suddenly and ran to the bathroom. She vomited violently and began to cry. She cried for

---

[11]Play Audio: "Walk Unafraid" by R.E.M.

what seemed to her like hours, only stopping to vomit again. Still sobbing, she lay her head down on the bathroom floor and fell back asleep.

A half hour later, Karen was awoken from her bathroom respite by the ringing of her telephone. Reluctantly, she hoisted herself from the floor and went to the kitchen to retrieve the phone.

"Hello?" Her voice was shaky.

"Miss Karen Davis?" inquired the voice on the other end.

"Speaking."

"Karen, there's been an incident. Can you please come to the Courtsdale Police Department?'

"What's this all about?" Karen asked.

"I'm not at liberty to discuss this matter over the phone, ma'am. You'll be briefed when you come in. Please be advised this is an urgent matter."

Karen hung up the phone, unable to respond. *Something's happened to John*, she thought. As she dressed and drove to the police station, she was *almost* surprised at her inability to cry, despite her sureness that something horrible had happened. Still, her lack of tears *did not* surprise her; she'd already run out of tears for the day.

Twenty-Three

The drive downtown passed quickly. She'd received her wakeup call from the police department a few minutes before seven o' clock, allowing her to miss the peak of morning rush-hour traffic. With her mind racing aimlessly from one horrible thought to another she paid little attention to driving, let alone to the time it took for her to arrive at her destination. When she finally did arrive at the police station she quickly rushed inside, not even bothering to lock her car doors. She was parked in the police department's lot, after all.

Upon entering the building, Karen made a straight line for the main information desk. The woman working was short and round with a mop of permed hair upon her head that had recently fallen victim to a horrendously bad dye job. A pair of thick-rimmed plastic glasses perched upon her nose.

"Hello, can I help you?" Karen had expected her voice to be nasal and whiny, but instead it was startling smooth – almost sensuous. As she spoke Karen recognized her voice as the woman who'd called her earlier that morning.

"Yes. Yes you can help me. At least I hope you can help me," Karen replied spastically. "I think you called me this morning. I mean, I know the police department called me this morning but I think you were the actual person to call me. Did you call me?" Her words were precariously close to one another, almost jumbled in her rush to get them out.

"Well ma'am, that depends," the woman responded slowly. "First I need to know your name. If you can give me your name, then I can attempt to give you an answer."

"Karen," she sputtered. "Karen Davis. My name is Karen Davis."

"Karen Davis… let's see here." The woman ran her fingers through a stack of papers, apparently looking for notes to clue her in as to who this crazy 'Karen Davis' character was. "What time did you say we called you? It was this morning, right?"

"Yes, it was this morning. About a half an hour ago, like 6:45 or so?" Karen continued to wait as the woman continued to remember why they would have called. She strived to look behind the front desk to see if she recognized anyone who might help give her a more immediate answer. "Come on, you have to remember me. You just called like twenty minutes ago for Christ's sake!"

"Now, now ma'am. There's no reason to get snippy. I'm simply making sure I get you the correct – ah, here it is. Yes, I did call you earlier. If you'll just take a seat, I'll inform you when they're ready."

"When who's ready?" Karen was exasperated. "I don't even know what happened or why you called me here! Can't you at least tell me that?"

"I'm sorry ma'am," the woman replied politely, "but I really don't know the answer to that. If you'll wait here Lt. Pickerson should be with you shortly. I've been told he's in his car now and should be arriving any minute. It shouldn't be long."

"Ugh." Karen sighed heavily and reluctantly took a seat in the lobby area. She absent-mindedly picked up a copy of the nearest magazine, which happened to be *Entertainment Weekly*, and began reading a feature article on the acting prowess of George Clooney. Her eyes moved quickly as she read the words, but in her mind she could think of nothing but the speculation of unknown events that brought her here so early on what would otherwise be another forgettable Thursday morning.

After only five minutes of waiting, the front doors opened and a tall, rather disagreeable looking man in a cheap charcoal suit entered. The woman behind the desk glanced up at the man.

"Lieutenant Pickerson, there's a Karen Davis here to see you," she said, pointing to Karen.

Karen stood up and offered to shake his hand. Pickerson ignored the gesture.

"Miss Davis, I'll be with you in just a bit." He then returned to the door, speaking to someone outside, "Take him down to Room B and I'll be down there in a bit. I don't want you asking him any questions until I get there, you hear me Detective?"

"Now, Miss Davis," he said, turning once again to face Karen. "I'm sorry to have kept you waiting. Were you waiting long?"

Karen was about to answer when he continued, "I'm afraid I have some very bad news, but I'd prefer to explain this all in my office. Would you please come with me?"

As she nodded in agreement Pickerson turned and started toward his office. Karen bent down to pick up her purse from her seat, stopping as she heard the front entry open again. She froze as she saw Miles enter, leading a handcuffed Steven. A second officer followed, and Karen's purse dropped to the floor.

"Steven? What's going on?" Karen asked as a look of shock streaked across her face. "Steven, Steven!"

Miles stopped and motioned for the other officer to continue on with Steven. As Steven passed Karen he looked into her pleading eyes and said nothing. He then turned his gaze to the floor and continued past her, down the long hallway.

Miles reached his hand out to Karen and placed it gently on her shoulder. "I'm sorry, Karen," he said. "I'll take care of this. I'll get this all straightened out." Then he too turned and continued down the hallway.

"Miss Davis? I'm waiting." It was Pickerson. Still in shock, Karen reached again for her purse and followed the Lieutenant to his office. She didn't dare ask a thing until she received some sort of explanation for just what the hell was going on.

Pickerson's office was tucked neatly away in the back corner of the third floor's homicide unit. His desk was an unusual array of documents waiting to be filed, empty pizza boxes, and half-filled cups of coffee. Somewhere beneath the mess was his computer. She waited in silence as he turned the machine on and waited for it to boot up.

"Now, Ms. Davis, I've been told you were in attendance at the AH-DATA gala last night." His manner of speaking was robotic, as if he were somehow uncomfortable talking to Karen. She noticed his eyes wander from her face down to her breasts.

"Ahem," Karen brought his attention back to her face. "Yes, I was there last night. I went with John Paluniak, but I'm sure you already know that. Would you mind telling me exactly what I've been called in here for?"

"Oh God, no one told you," he said – half muttering. "Well Karen – can I call you Karen? I'm extremely sorry to have to be the one bringing you bad news, especially so early in the morning…" his voice trailed off.

"I'm already expecting the worst, Lieutenant. Now if you'd just be so kind as to *tell me* just what this bad news is, I'd be a little happier."

"Right… well, this morning we found the body of John Paluniak at his downtown office. It appears to be a homicide. Actually, we're certain it was a homicide."

"Oh my God," Karen gasped. She'd already known in her heart that something bad had happened to either John or Steven, but that one of them had been killed - she still didn't believe it. Now that she was faced with the direct truth from a source other than her woman's intuition, however, she was forced to accept it. "Do you… know who did it?" she asked.

"We have a suspect in mind, but there's nothing definitive yet. Do you have any reason to suspect anyone, Karen? From what we've gathered, you and John were pretty close. Was there anyone you knew who might have harbored ill intent towards him? Did he have any enemies you were aware of? Anyone who might have wanted to harm him?"

"No one that I can think of," she replied. "He was a pretty well-liked guy. In fact, last night he seemed to be the most-respected man I'd ever met."

"Again, I'm sorry to have to bring up bad ideas and possibilities, but I have to ask…" Pickerson hesitated, looking to the floor for a few seconds before continuing, "Was your boyfriend, Steven Carvelle, how do I say this… friendly, towards John?"

"Well, they did have their differences, Lieutenant. But I know Steven, and there's no way he would have hurt John, let alone kill him, if that's what you're implying." Karen's faced tightened at the realization of the implied accusation. She was tempted to get up from her chair and leave Pickerson's office, but somehow constrained herself and remained seated. "That *is* what you are implying, isn't it?"

"I can't lie to you Karen; we have serious reason to believe your boyfriend may be responsible for the death of John Paluniak. And from what you and others have told us, the two were not friendly toward one another. That's even more reason to believe he could be involved."

"Pardon my French, Lieutenant, but fuck you. Fuck you. Steven may not be the most sensitive man in the world, but I sure as fuck know him well enough to know he's not a killer. Where do you get the nerve to even think something like that? And what kind of person do you think I am? Do I look like the kind of woman who would be the girlfriend of a cold-blooded killer? Fuck you and your accusations! I hope you're done asking me questions, because I'm leaving. Thank you Lieutenant."

Karen stood quickly from her chair, knocking over a coffeepot on the desk beside her as she did so. She grabbed her purse and opened the door. Before she could leave, however, Pickerson added one final word.

"We never said it was intentional, Miss Davis." *So now it's Miss Davis,* Karen thought. "Oh, I forgot to mention – his son is being held downstairs on the second floor day-care center. His aunt Alana has been awarded temporary custody and should be in town tonight to pick him up. We've told her she can pick him up at your work. Would you mind taking him with you?"

Oh shit... I forgot all about Dakota, she thought as tears began to stream down her face. Apparently she still had a few tears left in reserve from this morning, saved up for horribly sad occasions such as this. "Fine," she muttered as she walked out of Pickerson's office.

The descent in the elevator to the second floor was marred with introspection and self-doubt. She'd dreaded hearing what Pickerson had told her since she'd been so abruptly woken, but what she dreaded even more was the inevitable wretchedness of looking into Dakota's eyes when she would finally meet up with him in room beyond. She felt ashamed at her hopes the police had already explained to Dakota what had happened. He deserved to hear this abysmal news from someone close, but her confidence cowered at the thought of having to do it herself. Would he even really understand what had happened? Would Dakota really understand that, like his mother, his father too would never be coming home? She wiped her eyes on the sleeve of her jacket and opened the door to the Courtsdale daycare unit, a.k.a. hell.

"Karen Davis?" A stout African-American woman in her early fifties welcomed her immediately as she entered the room. "Hello Karen, Lieutenant Pickerson said you'd be coming." The woman cupped Karen's hands in her own, her eyes were wet with unshed tears of her own. "It's a horrible thing, what happened. I'll let you know we've had some time to talk to Dakota about it; but we're not quite sure if he really understands or not. He understands that his father's dead, God bless him, but he hasn't cried or anything of the sort. We're worried he's in some sort of mental shock or denial, or something..." her voice trailed off. "Anyway,

I'll go get him for you. He's been asking for you all morning – wondering when 'Aunt Karen' was coming in to take care of him."

"Yes, yes that'd be fine." It was all Karen could say.

In less than a minute the woman returned to the room. Her right arm was pulled behind her, down a corridor. As she slowly came into the room, Karen could see she had Dakota in tow. The first thing Karen noticed were his eyes – they were glazed over and empty. As he moved his eyes to meet hers she was taken aback by their lack of *anything*. The boy looked to be in shock, but as Karen began to speak he stopped her suddenly.

"Please Aunt Karen, not now."

She was shocked by the maturity (or immaturity) of his denial to speak about the situation. "Dakota, we're going to go to the daycare and then you'll hang out with me until your aunt comes to pick you up. Is that all right?"

"Yeah," he replied almost, almost angrily. He then grabbed her hand tightly and led her out of the room.

Twenty-Four

"Damn you Miles. I can't believe you had me frickin *arrested.* You know as well as I that I didn't do anything to Paluniak. Shit, you know *better* than I do, since I was too damned drunk to even piss straight last night." Steven and Miles were sitting in the front lobby of the police department, where Karen had seen him earlier. The handcuffs previously shackling his wrists were gone; he and Miles were talking as friends again.

"I know that, Steven. And you know I know. There's a reason you're a free man already; once I explained to Pickerson how sloppy-ass drunk you were last night he realized the possible media-fiasco he could have on his hands. Well, that and the fact I told him I took the keys to your ignition before I left you. You know, so you wouldn't go drive off and do anything stupid?"

"You took my fucking car keys? Jesus H. Christ, man, what if there had been some sort of major emergency?"

"Would you come off it already?" Miles lowered his voice to a whisper, "No, I didn't take your damn keys. I told him I did; there's a difference. You had better keep your mouth shut about it though man because if *anyone* finds out I lied about something like that, my ass is out the door. Next thing you know, my family'll be moving into *your* place."

Miles chuckled at the thought of his family crowded into Steven's paltry dwellings.

"Whatever. Well, I suppose I should thank you then. So… thank you." Steven looked up from his conversation at the empty lobby. "Man this place sure is dead in the mornings. And where the hell is Karen anyway? I thought you said Pickerson was already done talking to her."

"Yeah, he finished up with her just before I got there. I even saw her getting into the elevator on the way to pick up the kid. I'm sure she'll be here any second, just give her some time. I'm sure it's a lot to deal with; you know what I mean?"

"Yeah, I suppose you're right. I'll tell you one thing though, I'm happy as hell I'm not stuck in her shoes. I'd rather get arrested under false pretenses than have to tell a kid his dad's dead any day."

"Steven – a little respect?" As he spoke, Miles pointed to the side corridor leading to the main elevators. Even with the poor lighting from a burnt out light bulb Steven could make out little Dakota, with Karen bringing up the rear.

"Hey Karen," Steven had to be careful about what he said so he wouldn't offend her accidentally. This was a touchy situation, one he decided best dealt with by the eggshell approach. "Karen, you okay honey?" She ignored him and continued walking.

"Karen, I know this is hard for you. Would you please talk to me? I'll do whatever I can to help." Steven's words held a hint of supplication.

"Don't you get it Steven?!" Karen spun to face Steven. "I don't want to talk to you. I don't want to talk to anyone right now. You want to help me? You leave me the fuck alone, you bastard!" Miles grabbed Dakota's hand from Karen and led the boy outside. Karen continued to address Steven. "I woke up this morning and I knew that all my shit was fucked up, and I knew you had something to do with it. I just got done talking with Pickerson and he said you're the one who did this! Shouldn't you be locked up? How can they even let you out?"

"Karen, baby, I didn't do anything – I swear. It was all a misunderstanding; they let me go because they realized I'm just an innocent drunk! How dare you even *think* there's any credence to what Pickerson tells you?" Steven's voice was rising steadily. "You *know* me Karen. I'm the man who loves you!" Steven was yelling. "I'd think you could afford me at least the respect to know I'm not a fucking killer!"

Karen turned from Steven and continued to the exit. Steven continued to berate her.

"What the fuck Karen? You aren't even going to talk to me? This shit isn't just about you, you know."

Karen stopped and turned. "No, it's not just about me. It's about a little boy of whom I've suddenly been thrust the responsibility of. And no, I'm not going to talk to you Steven. You're not even talking; you're yelling. Ta-ta." And she was gone.

The door shut behind Karen and Steven became suddenly aware of the spectacle he'd become. He became aware of his surroundings, but mostly he became aware of the onlookers who'd joined him in the room. One person in particular caught his attention.

"No fucking way..."

Twenty-Five

The basement office of the coroner was dark, save for a lone lamplight which broke through the back shelves. Tucked behind rows of dusty medical manuals and jars containing various human organs marred with every disease and disorder imaginable, was a makeshift office. The lamp perched on the end of a filing cabinet threw a dismal glow; dust and shadows danced recklessly as the cabinet drawer slammed shut.

"I don't really care about that, you hear me? All I care about is getting what I've got rightfully coming." Jeffrey's hoarse voice tore through the stale air as he reprimanded the person on the other end of the phone.

"Okay, well in that case I've got an update for you. They've already brought in our latest. No, I haven't seen it yet, but from what I've heard he ain't pretty." He paused. "No, don't mess with the face again, after what happened last time you think that's smart?" Another pause. "Right, well I can get you her name but that's about it. Likely she'll be in town this afternoon. I don't have anything more for you now, but as always you're going to be the first to know. You just better keep things a bit lower profile from here on out, because if I *ever* get caught for this yours will be the first name I mention."

The light cast ghastly shadows across Jeffery's face; his anger magnified tenfold in the shadows. He pulled the phone from his ear and gently placed it back in its cradle on the desk beside the cabinet. Reaching for the cabinet, his hand stopped on the manila folder resting next to the lamp. His other hand reached for the lamp switch and, as he returned the room to darkness, the name on the file flashed across his eyes, its reflection shining for a split-second as the shadows swallowed him. *Paluniak, Jonathan Matthew*, it read.

He sat in the darkness for some time, not saying a word. He remained there until the gentle click-clack of approaching footsteps echoed from the hallway. Just as the footsteps reached the entryway he switched the lamp back on, tucking Paluniak's file into his left armpit. His dark eyes glistened in this new bath of light. Until he blinked the tears away, that is.

"Hello? Is there anyone here?" Jeffery didn't recognize the voice. "Franklin, are you down here?" The lights in the main room flickered to life.

"I don't think he's here, man. Didn't you say he'd be here?" Jeffrey prayed for whomever they were to leave.

"Yeah, that's what he said at least. Oh well, I bet the old butcher'll be here any minute. Let's just stick around a bit and see if he shows."

Damn, Jeffery thought. *I might as well go and see who it is before they just wander back here*. "Hello!" Jeffrey forced the most earnest voice he could muster. "I'll be right out. I'm just preparing a file. Franklin ain't here yet though."

"Jeffrey, that you? It's Detective Miles. I've got Steve Carvelle here with me too."

Sweet Mother of Mary, these folks are the last people I want to see this morning.

"Detective Miles talked to Franklin and he said we should meet him down here to go over some of the primary findings on the Paluniak murder. You hear anything about that?"

"Yessir, that's who's file I'm getting together."

"Jesus, I hate coming down here when it's just him. I just can't stand his attitude, it's like it would kill him to talk to someone. He's got to learn some social skills or something."

Miles tried not to laugh. "Quiet Steven," he whispered. "Someday you're going to say something you regret and I'm not going to be around to save you."

I can hear you, you know, thought Jeffrey. *I'd give you a piece of my mind too, if I thought it would do any good.*

"Good morning gentlemen! I see you beat me here. Doughnut?" Franklin entered the room with a box of Dunkin' Donuts in his hand. He was followed by two EMTs pushing a gurney with a black zippered body bag on top.

At the sound of Franklin's entrance, Jeffrey emerged from his back office. "Picking up or dropping off?" he asked the shorter man. He looked at Jeffery quizzically. "I'm just fooling with you, son!" Jeffery's laugh was like an old vacuum, torn with age and a few hundred cigarettes too many. "Anyway, I'll take it from here. A good day to you both."

"Thanks Jeffrey. Prep him like usual, we're gonna dig right in here I think. These boys look like they've got places to go!"

"Actually…" Miles began. Steven stopped him before he could say any more.

"Ha ha!" Franklin chuckled. "I know Steven, you don't want to have to be here any longer than you have to be. This wasn't pretty – I wouldn't blame you if you ditched on out already."

"No, it's alright. I'm about as prepared as I think I can be. After seeing him this morning all posed and cut up, this will be a cakewalk." Steven wasn't very good at lying, and he knew it. "Actually, could you get me a bucket? You know, just in case?" he asked, his face blushed with shame.

"You know, there's no reason you have to actually *watch* the autopsy, Steven," said Franklin. "It'll turn out the same either way, and you'll probably get the results from Miles as soon as I send them over anyway. You guys can go do whatever if you like."

"Yeah Steve, let's get out of here. I don't think I can even handle watching this one. What I saw earlier was enough for me." Miles grabbed Steven's sleeve roughly and pulled Steven with him toward the door.

"I actually would like to know what happened as soon as possible, Miles. You know Karen is going to be asking me about it as soon as she talks to me next." *If she talks to me, that is.*

"Steven…" Miles was getting fidgety. "I *really* don't want to stick around for this. You can stay if you want, but I'm not."

"Why don't you two just wait out in the hallway?" Franklin interjected. "There's a bench out there where you two can sit while I do this. I'll be out as soon as I have some preliminaries for you. How's that sound?"

Steven grabbed Miles by the arm and started toward the door. "Let's go." A rush of relief ran through Steven's blood and he felt his body ease back into itself. *Thank God we don't have to watch one of these again.*

From the hall they could hear just about everything that went on in the adjacent room. They did their best to ignore the resultant sounds, including the deafening thud as Paluniak's body was moved to the cutting board.

"So," Miles spoke first, and then hesitated. "What was the deal with Tremel earlier? For a second there I thought I might have to arrest you for real."

Earlier that morning, as Karen and Steven fought in the downstairs lobby of Courtsdale PD, a crowd of onlookers amassed eager to listen in on their argument. Sure, they didn't exactly gather around the two in a circle, but still they craned their necks just enough to get that extra earful, making sure not to appear so obvious to let on they were devouring the spicy conversation like a plate of Szechuan beef. Like any rubberneckers, the appearance of disaster was enough to draw their interest, and that's what Steven felt he and Karen were quickly becoming: a grisly car wreck of a relationship, a two car pileup that would claim at least one, if not both of their lives if one of the two didn't stop driving so offensively.

Of course like any disaster waiting to happen, the media were waiting perched in the trees ready to swarm like vultures at the first sign of death's looming shadow. The most impenitent of this flock, at least in Steven's experience, was Mary Tremel, the lead reporter at Channel Four News.

"Tremel's on time, with this breaking news at nine." This was the tagline that'd become synonymous with a Tremel story. Channel Four had used it for years, and despite its unbelievably cheesy nature, it never failed to bring in a healthy helping of viewers. If it was breaking news and Tremel covered it, it was sure to be fantastic. She had a penchant for making things much more extraordinary and dramatic than they were. She was a sensationalist straight to the bone and Steven held no respect for her or her reporting "style."

Their paths had crossed more times than Steven could hope to remember, and more times than he could wish to forget. Mostly their embattlements arose over stories they were both covering. As a newspaper reporter, Steven held a deeper sense of pride in his work and his medium. Television, he thought, was too face-paced and commercial-driven to be an effective news medium. The emphasis was always on the story that brought in the highest ratings, and stringing the viewer along throughout the program with "important updates to follow" was just a way to keep the advertising dollars rolling in for the entire length of the broadcast. This was why "Tremel's on time…" was such an effective tactic, and why it grated Steven's nerves to a pulp so frequently.

When Steven approached a story his goal was to get the facts first and worry about the presentation later. It was his job to report the news, not to spin it in any way, shape or form. At least that was how he approached his work in the past. Recently a feeling of despair had filtered its way into his blood. Unlike many in his position, however, Steven's desperation didn't lie in an internal feeling of helplessness. He'd seen many before him crack under the pressures of reporting what ultimately boiled down to horrifically disparaging news of the tumultuous downfall of world culture.

No, his distraction came from the feeling that no one really *cared* any more about what went on in the world. Newspapers were losing their voice to the exciting and entertaining world of television news broadcasts. Sure, television news had been around for years, but in this world of 24/7 news there was a new need to *entertain* the audience to keep ratings high which in turn kept the dollars rolling in. People were no longer interested in what was going on in the world around them. The world around them had ceased to exist and all people really cared about was what would be on next on "that CNN show."

Mary Tremel wasn't to blame for society's sudden change in attitude, and Steven knew that. But still, Tremel wasn't helping matters much and Steven felt more and more like he was becoming the world's fatalistic martyr, only unlike Joan of Arc, his faith was slowly dying.

That morning, when Steven and Karen exchanged their pointed words with sharp tongues in front of a company of strangers Steven had been so preoccupied in the immediate situation that he failed to notice the world around him. If he had, he might have noticed that the center of that world was on Mary Tremel and her news crew. She had undoubtedly heard through some sort of police-scanner-grapevine that Steven had been brought in to the station for something to do with this new murder. Mary and Steven's animosity was hardly one-sided, and each one's abhorrence for its doppelganger functioned as fuel for the other.

"Mr. Carvelle, can I get a moment of your time." Mary always asked people's permission before she started her interrogations, but not once did she pay mind to their reply. So it only made sense that she'd disregard Steven's response as well.

"Mary, I don't have time for this right now. Will you please go away?" he had responded.

"I'll let you be after you answer a few quick questions for our viewers," she interjected. "Is it true that you are being questioned for the murder of John Paluniak?"

"I told you already Ms. Tremel, I have nothing to say. Now if you'll excuse me…" Steven pushed Tremel aside with his shoulder and left the building through the front doors. This didn't stop his growing entourage, however. Tremel, her cameraman, and a group of nearly twenty onlookers rushed out the door behind him.

"Mr. Carvelle, is it true that you have no alibi for last night and that you felt Mr. Paluniak was having an affair with your girlfriend?"

Steven's patience had already dissipated long ago; he'd started his day by being witness to the aftermath of an acquaintance's grisly murder, been hauled to the police station and questioned as to his involvement in said murder, and been confronted by his girlfriend (with whom he was already in less than spectacular standing) about his involvement in the murder. *And now this bitch wants to broadcast me all over damnation as a primary suspect?* Steven's patience had fled.

"Turn that fucking camera off right now or I'll have you sued for slander. You think you're the top of the fucking planet, but you're not. You're just some cunt who's sensationalized her way to where she is. You don't give a fuck about what's really going on, do you? You sit there with your fancy outfit and layers of makeup and you walk like you're Hollywood. And you know what? You are Hollywood. You're not real and you'd better hope to hell that your "viewers at home" never figure that out."

Steven was yelling now, and had long since grabbed the microphone from Tremel's hand. He had moved in on her, and on the concrete staircase leading to the front entryway of the Courtsdale Police Department, he had made her cower. His words were shouted into the microphone, and she could feel his hot breath on her face as the words erupted.

As the vocal outburst subsided, he raised the microphone above his head quickly and Tremel shielded her face with her hands to protect it from the forthcoming blow. Steven brought his arm down with nearly as much force as Thor's hammer. The microphone shattered on the step next to the woman, sending splinters of plastic across the concrete. He dropped the microphone's metal skeleton into Tremel's hands and walked to his car as everyone else, including Miles, looked on in shock.

"Oh, that? That was just some steam that had to be let off. No big deal," Steven replied to Miles. "I just had a rough day already and she wasn't helping matters."

"Well you're just damn lucky you didn't hit her or she would have had you on battery, no questions asked – especially since she had the camera on. *That*, you would have been arrested for."

"Yeah, well she was invading my space. What I'm worried about is what happens when they broadcast that shit on the news today."

"I wouldn't worry about that too much. They don't have permission to shoot footage inside the police department, and when they started their little interview with you they were inside. I confiscated the tape from the camera guy after you left; threatened to arrest them if they didn't turn it over."

"And they actually listened to you?" Steven was awestruck.

"Well, I also had to promise a short exclusive interview with Tremel regarding this case for News at Nine tonight."

"So basically you saved my ass."

"Basically."

"I suppose I should thank you."

"Wouldn't hurt."

Twenty-Six[12]

The view from Alana Harcourt's taxi window was bleak, even though the sun was shining brightly in a nearly cloudless sky. Given the news of her brother's death earlier that morning, however, not even sunshine days could lift her spirits past where they currently lay.

She'd been at work when she received the phone call. Her secretary told her it sounded urgent; Alana told her to take a message. As the art director for Paraffin Media, a leader in corporate design and architecture in Chicago, she had relatively little time for "urgent" calls, unless they came from above. And in those instances it was much more likely she'd be contacted through her direct line. Besides, she was set to meet with her directors shortly to discuss third quarter numbers.

Her secretary buzzed again. "No, Alana. You *have* to take this."

You have to take this… the words reverberated through her as the taxi turned left onto Water Street. *Why did I have to take it? Why did I*

---

[12]Play Audio: "Suddenly Everything Has Changed" by The Postal Service

even have to get that call? she thought. *This is going to change everything.*

Three years ago she'd been Alana Paluniak. Within a few more weeks, she'd return to that name, but she'd never be Alana Paluniak again. Not the same person she was three years ago, at least. An abusive relationship can only last so long. It lasts much less when the abuser is unemployed and you're on the fast track. Alana learned this the hard way, and was in the midst of a messy divorce (*when isn't it messy*, she thought) and would soon be back to a somewhat recognizable life.

She'd been promoted heavily since taking an internship at Paraffin shortly after completing her Master's in Design, so financially she'd be set. She'd be a single woman again, with endless opportunities, her own last name, and none of the burdens of Matthew.

I lose one saddle only to gain another. Damn it John, why did this have to happen? She sobbed quietly in the back seat, hoping the driver wouldn't take notice. If he did, she hoped he'd at least spare her the questions.

"The Northwest Gate, please," she managed to mutter as the car neared O'Hare International Airport. The driver nodded, remained silent.

What am I going to do now? I don't know how to deal with this. I mean, he was my only brother. This is rough enough losing him. God, I don't even want to think about how I'm going to explain this to Dakota. I wonder if he even understands what's going on... that his father's never coming home.

The phone call from Courtsdale Police Department didn't offer many details as to her brother's death. All she could recall was being told her brother had been killed the night before, and that it would be best if she came down right away. She'd obviously be the one to deal with most of the proceedings from here on out: the funeral, taking care of the will, taking care of Dakota.

It's been almost a year since I even saw that little boy. I wonder if he'll even remember who I am. She felt her nose begin to run.

"Here we are, the Northwest Gate. That'll be $45.10 please."

Alana paid the driver and retrieved her luggage from the car's trunk. In her rush she'd only brought one bag; she could pick up whatever else she needed once she figured out what was going on. As she entered the terminal she took note of the clock on the wall. Her flight was set to leave at 2:45: twenty minutes to spare. It'd feel like hours.

Twenty-Seven

After several hours of excruciatingly boring cutting, prodding, poking and observing, Steven and Miles had decided they weren't about to learn anything new about the Paluniak murder and decided to duck out early. Nothing new had been uncovered, other than what had already been ascertained from the scene itself, and Steven personally felt better off not seeing any more gruesomeness than was absolutely necessary.

Earlier, Miles dropped Steven off downtown at Paluniak's building so he could retrieve his car, so Steven and Miles had driven to the city morgue separately. Both had parked their cars in the public parking structure on Fairfield, two streets over. The easiest way to the Fairfield ramp, however, was to cut through the morgue's back alley which, although reeking of the odor of used medical equipment from the morgue's dumpsters, remained a fairly well-kept route. The truth was it enjoyed a relatively small amount of foot traffic and that it was downtown city property ensured that the city's cleaning crews gave special care to it. Had it *not* been so clean, nor had Steven the benefit of a personal police escort, he would still rather have taken the long way around. An alleyway was by no means a safe place to be, even in the light of day. Steven had reported on his fair share of muggings and whatnot in these threatening recesses of the city, albeit those had been in an earlier, darker time in Courtsdale's past.

Yet, as the two men made their turn from the building's front façade into this less-illustrious path, they stopped short. Up ahead was a parked car – which was illegal for one thing, but also a bit out of place. A black Cadillac had no business in a morgue's alley.

Miles pulled Steven back, behind a dumpster against the outer wall of the morgue. "Shh" he pantomimed, putting his finger to his lips.

Up ahead, out of their view, Steven could make out the sound of a heavy door opening. Footsteps were barely audible above the sound of the idling vehicle. Miles put his hand on Steven's chest. "Stay put," he whispered, as he poked his head slightly around the front of the dumpster.

After less than a minute of impatient waiting, Steven heard the door to the morgue open and close again. The vehicle was put into gear, and the sound of tires slowly moving on asphalt followed.

Miles turned to Steven. "You go on ahead. I have to check something out."

"What? What's going on? Who was that?" asked Steven.

"Just go home or something. I'll catch up with you later. There's something I need to do quick… just in case."

Twenty-Eight

For Steven, the evening couldn't have come soon enough. The hours spent stewing about his apartment waiting for Karen to come over from work had been completely unproductive. She'd called him earlier, around four o' clock, to let him know she'd be getting there late, and to remind him that she was still not happy to have been pulled into an investigation revolving around the death of her best friend and the supposed involvement of her own boyfriend.

"I'm not going to be able to make it to your apartment as early as I thought, Steven. Dakota's Aunt Alana's flight doesn't come in until later and she's not going to be able to pick him up today. I'm going to have to watch him tonight, so I have to pick up some dinner for us on my way home. Do you want to come over and keep us company?"

"Why don't you bring him over here? I can make dinner for all of us," said Steven. "I didn't have any plans tonight other than to sit around here anyway. If you want to come hang out, I'd really appreciate it though. I've had a pretty rough day."

Karen hesitated, then replied "You've had a rough day? I'm sure it was horrible for you… what with being arrested for no reason, then released, free to go about your business. I mean, my best friend was found *mutilated* this morning, and I'm stuck taking care of his son, but hey – no big deal." Her speech was quickening, growing more agitated as she continued "Yeah, you've had a rough day. I feel *so* sorry for you, Steven. I really do."

"Jesus Karen, I know today has been rough for you too. You know what I meant," he responded defensively. "I meant we *both* could use some time together; forget about all of this crazy shit that's been going on. It's stressful on both of us."

"No – you don't get it. *I'm* stuck being a temporary mom for Dakota, Steven. I didn't ask for this. I mean, I adore him but this isn't my job. I'm freaking out here trying to keep all these kids under control while also trying to give this little boy the attention and nurturing environment he needs. I'm not qualified for this; it's not my problem. And his aunt? I don't even know her, other than that she's some sort of workaholic dealing with problems of her own. When she gets here Dakota's going to be tossed into another world altogether. And you know what? Good. I want to help him out, I really do… but this isn't my problem! You? You're not my problem either. I'm sick to death of having to deal with bullshit day in and day out and this is *way* beyond what I can handle."

"A temporary mom? It's just one night, Karen. Don't be so melodramatic," was all Steven could say.

"You know? You don't know shit about how I feel. You don't know how I feel on a normal day lately, and you sure as shit don't know how I feel today. And you know what else?"

"No Karen, I don't…"

She hesitated again, and fell silent.

"What Karen? What else?" Steven was quickly becoming bored of this conversation.

"Never mind."

"No, tell me. Tell me what else, Karen."

"When I think about … earlier. When they were questioning me about you…"

"What about it?"

Silence again. "Karen?"

"Like I said, never mind… We'll be at your place in a little while. I gotta go." And she hung up the phone.

Steven eyed the clock. It was already quarter to nine and Karen still had not shown up. He contemplated calling her at home, but decided against it for fear of upsetting her further. He really did just want to try to relax tonight: the two of them together, escaping all the madness of the past few days.

Nervously fidgeting, he began to search the apartment for his slippers, eventually locating them on the bathroom floor. He picked up the towel from his shower that morning, cringing slightly at the sight of blood caked onto the grout between the mildew-infested floor tiles. Opening the under-sink cabinet, he grabbed a bottle of bleach, poured a bit on the floor where the bloodstain resided and left the room to let the stain soak.

The ring of the doorbell throughout the silent apartment startled Steven, giving him a sudden awareness that he had been a bit more uneasy from his earlier escapades than he'd realized. When he opened the door, Karen stood in front of him looking more tired and worn than he could ever recall seeing her. As her eyes emerged from behind her weary eyelids, they appeared greased over - like a pair of glasses smeared by oily hands. Her hair, though tucked under her baseball cap, appeared flattened and matted to her skull contour. After a brief, unspoken exchange of hellos she entered the apartment and immediately collapsed onto the couch, turning on the television.

Steven broke the silence. "I wasn't sure you were coming. Where's Dakota?"

"He's with Beverly. She heard you and me talking earlier and told me she could watch Dakota tonight – that I needed some TLC too."

"How is he doing? Is he handling everything okay?" Steven did his best to appear compassionate. "I mean, I'm sure you did a great job taking care of him. I've seen how good you are with those kids. Plus I know you have a little bit of extra affection for that little guy."

"Well, he's taking it as best as he can. The thing is, I can't tell if he really understands what's going on. And to be honest, I don't know if he *should.* What a horrible thing to have happened… to never even know your mother and then to lose your father. Plus, it's not like someone can explain to him what *really* happened. It's too messed up for even me to accept or understand. The best way to get it across was just to explain that John was with mommy now and wouldn't be coming home. Ever."

The television cut to a commercial, a promo spot for the evening's news, drawing Steven's attention from the conversation. Noticing Steven's sudden lack of interest in what she was saying, she almost snapped at him – until she noticed the lead story.

"Tonight at nine: homicide in downtown Courtsdale. One of the city's finest is found murdered in the Liberty Mutual building. Be sure to tune in to Channel four for the latest. Tremel's on time with the news at nine!"

Rather than expunge upon his disgust for the sensationalistic advertisement, Steven responded to Karen's earlier comments. "That's just horrible, honey. I know how much John meant to you. Heck, he meant a lot to me just for meaning so much to you. I know he was a good friend, and I know you care about Dakota more than just about anyone else in the world. I'm sure you did more than enough just by being there for him."

"Yeah, I guess..." Karen's voice trailed off. "Hey, can we watch this? I know you don't like Tremel but I *really* want to see if they've found anything else out about what's going on."

Steven reluctantly nodded his head in agreement and joined Karen on the couch.

"This morning the body of prominent Courtsdale businessman and philanthropist, John Paluniak, was discovered in his office at Liberty Mutual in downtown Courtsdale," said the anchorwoman. "We go downtown to Mary Tremel, from a report filmed earlier today."

“Lisa, I’m standing outside Liberty Mutual, where the body of John Paluniak was found murdered early this morning. Police estimate he was killed sometime late last night, after attending the AHDATA gala at the Humphrey museum. Details are scarce, but police have alluded to a possible connection to the murder discovered earlier this week at the old Stengler Brewery.”

“How could they find a connection so quickly?” asked Karen, only to be silenced by a hush from Steven.

“Regardless of this possible connection, you can count on Mary Tremel to be there for the investigation of the heinous acts perpetrated by this demented madman. I had a chance to sit down and talk to one of the lead investigators on the case, Detective Miles Stanton.”

The camera cut to a view of Tremel and Miles at a desk.

“So detective, what can you tell me about these horrendous murders besieging our fair city?”

“Well Mary, an official link between the events of the last two days has not yet been established, although we are currently working under the assumption that the two murders are, in fact, connected. This is due to the elaborate amount of detail involved in each of these cases, as well as the fact that both share some thematic similarities.”

“What might those similarities be, detective?”

“I'm afraid I'm not currently at liberty to discuss specific details of the case. We're working up a profile, and we assure you, the person or persons responsible for this will be found, apprehended and brought to justice.”

The camera cut back to the story. "You heard it here first folks, The Courtsdale Coroner will be found, apprehended and brought to justice. Be sure to tune in to Channel Four tomorrow as we continue our coverage these atrocities, including an exclusive interview with Lieutenant John Pickerson when once again, Tremel's on time with news at nine!"

"What a load of sensationalist crap!" exclaimed Steven, turning off the television. "Did you notice how many times she mentioned her own name? And the Courtsdale Coroner – where on Earth did that come from? I've never heard Miles or anyone else call the killer or killers that! It's like she's *making up* news! What does a coroner have to do with anything? They don't kill people. Sure it's catchy, but why use alliteration if you're not making any sense?"

"I have to admit it Steven, you are right about that Tremel. I don't like her one bit," Karen chimed in. "She didn't even touch on the real story about who John was or even anything to do with the incident. It was like an ad for tomorrow's news."

"It's like she was just trying to hype up her follow-up story for tomorrow night," Steven continued, paying no attention to Karen. "She didn't even address the story. That's why I fucking hate TV reporters, especially that Tremel bitch. They always throw in their two cents and never keep things objective."

Karen sighed, realizing she'd been ignored once again. "I think I'm going to head out. It's been a long day and I have to work early tomorrow."

As she rose from the couch Steven interjected, "But you just got here."

“I know, but I have to work in the morning and you’re obviously upset so I don’t think this is going to be a very relaxing night anyway,” she said, opening the door. “I just really need to get some rest. I’ll talk to you tomorrow, okay Steven?”

Rather than beat a dead horse, Steven realized it would be best to just let her leave. After she left, Steven noticed a bit of pressure in his bladder. *Better take care of business* he thought, stumbling into the bathroom. As he relieved himself he felt a sudden burning sensation in the sole of his right foot. Looking down he realized to his dismay he’d been standing in a puddle of bleach that was slowly seeping its way into the still tender sore from when he’d cut his foot open in the shower the day before.

“Ouch!” he yelped, frantically pulling at his sock, then rinsing his foot off under the bathtub faucet.

Well, I know of at least one way to kill that pain, he thought as he hopped from the bathroom into the kitchen. Propped up against his countertop, he reached into the cupboard for a bottle of Jack Daniels, slid down to the floor and started drinking.

Feels better already.

the trouble with being god

Day Four

RESONANCE[13]

[13]Play Audio: "A Bad Dream" by Keane

the trouble with being god

Twenty-Nine

Death, murder, suicide – were they a means to an end or an end in themselves? Where does one go after the mortal coil is abandoned? Can one know a truth without having experienced it firsthand?

There was faith, and faith was fleeting. In a world of lies and deceit sprinkled lightly with fits of joy, wonder was ceasing. People had died, and people would continue to die. Was it someone's doing, or simply the end result of all the events that had transpired to date?

What good was faith in a world that seemed to be forever spiraling out of control? Where did fault lie? In the doer? In the victim? In an upbringing? Or perhaps in a flawed view of reality?

Am I the victim of circumstance?

How did I get to this point?

Can these events be stopped, or is it all set in motion?

Why won't this bitch die?

Patience, too, was fleeting. His arms heaved upward, then dealt a blow more furious than the sorrow of a loved one's passing. With an inspiring swell of relief, the sweat-soaked golf club in his hands expunged the remains of the expression below.

Karen faded, and Steven awoke.

Thirty

Keith Garret sat behind his desk in the corner office of the Channel Four studios, hastily studying his early reports of third quarter viewing habits. Numbers were up, but the summer was also winding down. The recent growth in viewership appeared to be nothing more than the annual result of people moving their daily activities indoors.

Warily, he followed the column down to the current week's initial viewer estimates. Although several programs had recently begun airing their new season, his expectations for growth from these developments only slightly interested him. He'd seen advance reels of several of the network's flagship shows, and was truthfully a bit worried. It seemed, to him, that recent programming had fallen into a bit of a slump of predictability and formula.

Not that Garret had a problem with these approaches to programming. In fact, when his bottom line was at stake, predictability and formula were often the best ways to make a buck in his business. People liked to see what they were comfortable with; anything that challenged them was too much work and likely to lead to further declines in viewing and therefore ad revenue.

Still, lately even Garret found the recent formulaic sitcoms or cop-dramas to be a bit too cookie-cutter. The fact that his parent network had been the last to jump on the bandwagon for these types of programming only led to further disappointment. His viewers who'd held interest in this type of programming had switched the channel long ago, and had already found their niche in the front-runners offered by his competiton years ago.

Nonetheless, as his finger followed the spreadsheet down the paper, the corners of his mouth turned up slightly. A grin took over his face.

Tremel, he thought, *you are a Godsend to this station.*

It had been his idea, months ago, to highlight one of their news reporters as the station's flagship program. There was nothing more interesting to local viewers than things that affected them personally, and local news continued to be the one area where Channel Four had never seen a drop in viewing. So, opting to throw a bit of the station's journalistic integrity out the window, Garret had promoted Mary Tremel to lead reporter.

For years Tremel had pushed for the spotlight. Earlier management had frowned upon her kiss-ass tactics, but had weathered them regardless since Tremel had never disappointed in her coverage of major news. Once Garret had been promoted to program manager, however, he pushed every internal channel he could to move Tremel up to the top of the totem pole.

Shifting the reports aside, Garret noticed a bundle of packages on the floor next to his desk. The two packages were wrapped in plain brown craft paper, tied together with a piece of jute string, one large enough to hold a basketball, with a much smaller one on top. A typewritten address was attached to the package.

FOUR YOUR EYES ONLY

ATTN: PROGRAM MANAGER
CHANNEL FOUR NEWS

411 WEST CUNNINGHAM

COURTSDALE

Garret opened the smaller of the two first.

Thirty-One

At 10:43 a.m. it had been exactly eight hours thirty minutes since Steven's life had resembled anything even vaguely familiar. Gazing dreamily into his bathroom mirror, he barely recognized his reflection. The man staring back at him was gaunt, his eyes sunken black and his left pupil slightly larger than the right. He needed to shave, but instead dropped to his knees and vacantly blotted the remaining bleach puddle from the floor with a wad of crumpled toilet paper.

How many times do I have to find out who I am? The answers seem to come to me and then disappear. I can't even feel my heart beat any more.

Where was Karen? Why had she left last night? Was she dead?

How many times would I have to beat her with a golf club to kill her? After ten blows would she be dead? Maybe just bloody and bruised. I wonder if a wood would do more damage than an iron. Could you split a skull with just one swing of a pitching wedge? I bet Arnold Palmer could do it.

He rubbed his eyes and cringed. He'd forgotten to rinse the bleach from his hands.

Well at least my eyes are clean. Now maybe I can see.

He went into the kitchen to make some breakfast and opened the refrigerator, finding only one egg in the carton.

Best if used by ... what day? Sunday? No – Monday. Everything expired on Monday.

He took the egg out of the carton, threw the empty box into the trash and grabbed a skillet from sink, giving it a quick rinse. Heat kills everything.

After a few minutes on the stove the pan was hot enough for cooking. He cracked the egg and dumped it into the hot pan.

My God, that smells. Fuck breakfast anyway.

Thirty-Two[14]

A pair of reading glasses, a pair of eyes and package sticky with blood lay on Garrett's desk. Next to it sat the larger, and still unopened, second box, which as a precautionary measure, the bomb squad had been called in to open.

Garrett himself stood slouched against the wall near the water fountain outside the front doors of Channel Four. The building had been temporarily evacuated while the police assessed the threat.

The black cop had asked him a lot of questions, but from what Garrett could tell he wasn't under any sort of suspicion. Still, he didn't know if he should stick around or go home. He figured he should probably stick around.

The stories they covered were always just that for him – stories. He hadn't ever spent any time in the field; he'd always been one step removed from the reality of everything... and now he was sure he liked it that way. Watching the horrors of everyday life unfold on the screen in front of him always had left him feeling safe and distant from the things

[14]Play Audio: "These Eyes" by The Guess Who

that had crept into the minds behind the faces shown every night on the news.

It was actually easier to remove himself from the reality of the things he saw *because* he saw them. He saw them like everything people see. Life was full of betrayals, murders and perversions. Most people paid to see them every day when they turned on their TVs or clicked on to the Internet. Celebrities were killers, killers were celebrities and none of it seemed real.

The eyes though, they *were* real. He recognized them the instant he saw them. He'd seen them thousands of times before. They stared at him from billboards, they told stories. There was nothing special about Mary Tremel's eyes. They were normal blue eyes, but he knew them as soon as he saw them staring blankly at him. They struggled to tell him a real story, but all he could see was their horror.

Thirty-Three

"I'm telling you John, we need to keep a tail on this guy. It's all there in my report. He's the one we should be watching."

Lieutenant Pickerson looked down at the police report in his hands and frowned. "Are you sure about this? Everything I see here is circumstantial. There's no physical evidence to back up any of your theory."

Miles defended himself. "Physical or not, I saw what I saw. Like I said, it's all there in the report. We need to get a warrant before it's too late."

"Just tell me what happened Miles. I don't feel like reading this right now, and I'd rather hear it all straight from you."

Miles sighed. "Fine, although I don't know why I even bother to fill out these reports anymore. It was yesterday afternoon; we were just leaving the morgue after the Paluniak autopsy ..."

"You go on ahead. I have to check something out."

"What? What's going on? Who was that?" asked Steven.

“Just go home or something. I’ll catch up with you later. There’s something I need to do quick… just in case.”

Steven paused, as if to argue, then said, “I'm going, but if this is important you have to promise to fill me in later.”

“Yeah fine, I promise. Now just go.”

Steven left, and Miles was alone, watching the idling Cadillac. Behind him he heard the lock on the basement access door to the morgue click open. He quickly moved to the opposite side of the dumpster and concealed himself in the shadows and trash that had accumulated.

Miles heard the door to the morgue open, followed by the clack of shoes on the wet asphalt. An African-American man approached the parked car, with his back to Miles and Miles's hiding spot. The window to the car rolled down and the man from the morgue and the man in the car started to talk.

“Is this it?” asked the man in the car.

The other man spoke, but it was impossible to hear the response from his current position. He saw the man's head nod, as he handed what appeared to be a manila envelope to the person in the Cadillac.

“So this is the latest, hm? Excellent work. Just excellent,” said the man in the car. “You said the next in line is Alana Paluniak? Our source in Chicago says she's on her way; we'll get to her first.

From inside the car came a hand holding a stack of cash. The man outside took the money, thumbing through it casually.

“A pleasure doing business with you, as usual,” said the man's gruff voice.

“Likewise,” came the voice from inside. “Now run along and let us know when the next one's ready and we'll pay the usual.”

The window to the Cadillac rolled up. Miles took note of the license plate as the car drove off. The man, left standing in the cloud of exhaust, turned and retreated to the morgue. As he turned, Miles caught a look at his face. As he had suspected from the voice, it was Jeffrey Harlen, the coroner's assistant.

“Like it says in my report,” Miles continued, “I immediately returned to the station to fill out a report on what I saw. I also tried to call you, but you were off duty and unavailable-”

“Never mind that. There's protocol for you to follow when I'm not available or can't be reached.”

“Right, and I followed it, which is why we're having this conversation to begin with. I requested a tap on his lines, and word has it that approval is just about to come through – along with a warrant to search his place. By this time tomorrow we should have him in custody, and we'll all be sleeping a little easier.”

“Don't rush on this, Miles. We need to know who was in that car. Did you run the plates yet?”

“I didn't have time myself, but I've sent down a request with my report. I should have an answer to that soon.”

“There's no rush. If the person in that car is in any way involved with this case, there's no way they'd be driving around with real plates. In the meantime, get to work on Harlen.”

Thirty-Four

The Keep wasn't any cleaner than the last time Steven and Miles had been there. In fact, Steven wasn't certain it had even been cleaned since their last visit. As he bellied up to the bar he noticed the reflexive actions his hands took to protect their master, gracefully avoiding any contact with the surely disease-ridden surface of the bar itself.

He was only one of three customers he could see, although there was a dark denim jacket slung over one of the stools at the end. The fourth guest was probably taking a leak. Despite his lack of competition for attention, it was almost five minutes before the bartender made any indication of recognizing he was there. The acne-scarred man took his order.

"Beer please."

"What kind?"

"Does it matter?"

As Steven took a long first drink he barely noticed how warm the beer was. He was surprised, however, at the time his watch showed: just after eleven in the morning. The beer was warm and it was barely past breakfast (for Steven at least). No wonder the place was so empty.

To tell the truth, I didn't even know bars were open this early. Maybe it's because of the neighborhood... or maybe it's because this place also serves food? Lunch hour is coming soon. Maybe it fills up with people on their lunch breaks. I certainly haven't been in here this early before. Normally I'd be at work, but I'm not really sure what that even means anymore. I don't even go to a job. Or maybe I'm always at work? Isn't that what I do? Observe and report? Always observing, always making mental notes for the future?

It doesn't really seem like I'm making many notes lately though. In fact, it's been really hard to remember much of anything. I can't even remember why Karen left last night.

Hell, I can't remember the last time she didn't leave.

The door to the bar opened, although no one paid it much attention. No one other than Steven, at least. Into the bar walked a woman, probably in her mid-thirties. She was pretty, with blue-grey eyes and long blond hair down past her shoulders. She was dressed conservatively: charcoal slacks and a long-sleeved black blouse. Steven stared toward her and their eyes met with a shared emptiness. She took the seat next to Steven.

"What are you having, miss?" asked the bartender gruffly.

"This gentleman next to me would like to buy me a scotch and soda," she replied.

"I would?" asked Steven, a bit incredulously.

"Well, if you wanted to fuck me you would."

Thirty-Five

How do stay-at-home moms do it? A constant one-on-one all day long? It's enough to drive someone crazy... or depressed. Or maybe depressed and crazy. I feel like I'm going crazy.

She took a last drag, stood up from the slide where she'd been sitting, dropped the cigarette and smothered the life from it with her foot. She didn't bother to pick up the butt, but did manage to kick some gravel up onto it.

"Karen," Beverly accosted her as she walked back in to the play room. "The cops called again while you were gone. They wanted to remind you that Ms. Paluniak's coming today to pick up Dakota."

"What? Did they think I'd somehow forgotten?" Karen replied sarcastically.

"I have no idea. I do know, however, that Dakota keeps asking where his daddy is though. I'm running out of things to say to him. The fact that he hasn't seen or heard from him since early last night is starting to have some realization kick in, or something. It's like separation anxiety, only it's more *empty* or something. Like he knows the anxiety won't ever let up." Beverly started to cry.

“Jesus Christ, Beverly,” Karen whispered, so the kids couldn’t hear her. “You're not going to help anyone by doing that. You don't think I'm having a hard enough time trying to do this as it is? We're watching, what, two dozen kids between the two of us, and I'm also supposed to somehow explain to Dakota that his daddy was butchered? And on top of it, I'm supposed to deal with my own feelings as well?”

Karen, allowing her desperation to get the better of her, yelled: “FUCK!”

Three kids started to cry. Dakota's face was blank.

“I'm sorry guys,” Karen said to the kids. “Karen's just a little sad today. You all know how it feels when you're sad, right?”

Libby Patterson, a four year old who'd only recently starting coming to their daycare dropped the doll she was playing with and stood up. She ran over to Karen, stopped short, looked into her eyes, and latched on to her leg with a big hug. Karen nearly started to cry, but she felt her heart swell and said “Thank you Libby.”

Beverly, in the meantime, had taken to calming the three criers. Karen made her way over to Beverly and took one of the children, a baby, in her own arms and rocked him gently.

“Did they say when she'd be coming?”

“No, they only said that she'd be here by the end of the day. I guess she came in from Chicago last night and said she'd pick Dakota up today, but didn't give them an exact time.”

“Well, hopefully it's sooner rather than later. I'm running out of things to tell him.” She paused. “I wonder if Dakota will like Chicago.”

Thirty-Six

The dream again. The cold concrete. The soft pale neck. The coppery taste of blood. Where did the gun come from? It's pressed firmly against her head, but where'd he get it? Flashes and thunder strike in his mind. It doesn't matter where. All that matters is that he has it now, and that she's scared. She'll feel him this time, and he'll taste her.

On the concrete the blood pools. *There'll be a stain there tomorrow, that's for sure.*

Who'll clean it up? Better make sure not to leave a personal trace. Damned DNA.

Such a pity to waste such a beautiful neck... to waste such a beautiful woman.

His gaze moves from the crevasse in her neck, to her sullied shoulders, stopping before the breasts. Thunder strikes again, but he's in the basement. Where is the thunder? Where is the lightning?

Another loud crack, and Steven wakes. A picture falls to the floor as the front door slams.

“Karen?” he called. “Is that you?”

Steven got up from the bed and made his way to the window, cracking the blinds slightly before closing them again, the glare of the mid-day sun too much for his eyes to adjust to in such short order. After a few seconds he regained his thoughts and the events earlier in the day began to take shape in his mind.

The woman from the bar really hadn't been all that special. She was at least five years older than he was, and even if he was single he really wouldn't have paid her much attention – not that being single ever stopped him from looking (or touching). Still, she held a kind of familiarity for Steven. Her blond hair held purity for him that he couldn't understand, and frankly didn't care about. The bigger question on his mind was whether she had been a good lay or not.

Regardless, she was gone now and he'd doubted he'd see her again. He picked up the phone and dialed.

“Where have you been?”

“You mean, *in whom* have I been?”

“I don't even want to know.”

“That's funny. I don't even know.”

Steven gave Miles a moment to break the silence with a laugh. The laugh never came.

“Steven, some serious shit has gone down today. More serious than everything else that's gone down, if you can believe it.”

“Don't tell me. Someone finally shut Tremel's mouth.”

"Actually, that's exactly what happened. Well, not exactly, but *exactly.*"

Another silence.

"Steven, we really need to talk. Can you meet me at The Keep in say, fifteen minutes? It's usually dead this time of day, and I need to speak to you in private."

"Sure; just give me a few minutes to take a shower."

"... and for God's sake, don't talk to anyone and definitely don't try to tell any more jokes."

"Yeah, yeah I'll be there soon, and I promise to be quiet," Steven replied. "But I'll do it for your sake and mine, not God's. Why I would do *anything* for something that doesn't exist is beyond me."

Thirty-eight minutes later, at 1:08 Steven arrived back at The Keep.

"Back so soon?" The acne-scarred bartender was still the only one working.

"Fuck off, asshole."

The bartender looked at the clock, back to Steven, and winked.

"What was that all about?" asked Miles.

"Just something you already told me not to talk to you about, and he obviously knows nothing about."

"If you're referring to *in whom you've been*, you're right, I don't want to know. What I do want to talk about is what you think is a joke. Or at least what you joke about. But there are some things you shouldn't joke about, and now there are definitely some things that you can't joke about – like the fact that Mary Tremel's head arrived at her office this morning, sans body."

"I'm not surprised," Steven replied nonchalantly. "The way she was carrying on about the murders, making them into some sort of show; she deserved what she got. Hell, she deserved it a long time ago. Now Garrett, that's a different story. He didn't necessarily deserve it, but he deserved a warning, which is what a head in a box is supposed to be."

"How did you know the box was sent to Garrett?"

"Who else would he send it to? The janitor? What I want to know are the details. The slimy, grisly, nasty details. What do you know?"

"I really don't know what to tell you, Steven. There aren't a lot of details yet. Early this morning we got a call from the station. It was pretty frantic, from what I heard, but basically they received two packages. Garrett opened one of them, and found a set of eyes and a pair of reading glasses inside. He contacted us immediately and told us about the second package. They sent a team out there, who took one look at the second box and called in the bomb squad. They opened it, finding Tremel's head inside."

"Whoever did it sure didn't care to leave any mystery about the eyes this time, did he? Although I do find it interesting that they were packaged separate from the head."

Miles nodded. "Yeah, we're not sure what to make of that either, but there's plenty of *mystery* here yet Steven, like … where's the rest of her?"

Steven thought about that for a minute.

"As for how the package got there in the first place, that's also unknown. It was sent directly to Garrett, but even though the postage all looked legit there's no way it could have gone through a real system. I mean, Tremel was on the news the day before, all in one piece. Not even overnight delivery could have gotten a package there that quickly, so we're pretty sure that however it got there it wasn't through the postal system. Still we're checking that out anyway, just in case our man's a pissed off postal worker."

"So that's it: a head in a box, bundled with eyes in a box, sent from the post office but not from the post office?"

"Actually, there's more. Her, uh, mouth was stapled shut. When they removed the staples they found a note inside. I can't remember exactly what it said, since I only overheard them reading it. Something like "Populist vault decapitate" or "decapitator." Decapitate? Off with the head? Sounds like some sort of Alice in Wonderland fantasy to me."

"Populus vult decipi, decipiatur?"

"Maybe that's it. I don't know. Could be."

"*The people want to be deceived. Let them be deceived.* It's something the Carlo Cardinal Caraffa said once about religion. Catholicism to be exact. He was a cardinal, and the nephew of Pope Paul the Fourth. Seems fitting for someone like Tremel, doesn't it?"

"What is that, Latin? I thought you said you don't know Latin."

"I don't, but it's one of my favorite quotes. I've always just felt it was a perfect example of the mindset behind religion, or in a broader sense, those who are in power. People like lies. They thrive on them because they can make their lives easier to understand. Why do I suffer? Because when I die I'll get a reward for my humility. It's a win-win situation, really. The poor idiots of the world all live in the delusion that ignorance is bliss, although they believe their ignorance to be knowledge. The ones who really have the knowledge are those who they worship, which aren't really gods any more than you or I are. They're the people in power, and for the most part people in power rely on religious institution to guide them in determining right from wrong and to give them purpose in their lives, when in reality our life's purpose is our own. But if you tell people that, they're not going to know what to do, so instead they feign ignorance and eventually believe the lies they're raised to uphold. Of course, the other reason I know what it means is because I killed Tremel."

Miles's frowned, and his voice took on a tone of complete seriousness. "Steven, I told you not to even joke anymore. They let you go the other day, but that doesn't mean they've lost interest in you. You're a suspect, whether you believe it or not – whether it even makes sense or not. You keep reporting on this story, just like Tremel did, and the more incompetence you point out the more my "buddies" downtown are going to try to drag you through the mud with them."

"Who said anything about a joke? Do you see me laughing? That stupid bitch deserved to die. I said it last night. Call Karen if you don't believe me. Throughout this whole mess everyone who's died has deserved it, as far as I'm concerned. They all spread lies or try to embrace the world of lies around us through complacency. The people want to be deceived? The people *don't* want to be deceived! They just don't know any better. Cut off a stupid reporter's head. Crucify a priest. Hell, I'd hang the Pope if I had the chance. These are evil people, Miles, and it's time to clean. The only time baptism is good is when there's soap involved; so you can call me Father Bubbles."

"What the *fuck* is wrong with you?" Miles was livid. "You're seriously messed up; did I ever tell you that? If you need help straightening your shit out, let me know. But in the meantime, there's some sort of mental disturbance in your system that needs to be cleared. I turn a blind eye to your hatred for religion, beliefs you know I hold a personal and spiritual attachment to, but when you start trying to claim you *killed* someone, that's beyond reproach."

"I did. I shot her in the chest four times, then I cut off her head and put it in a box."

"No you didn't. Like you said, you had some sort of mental failure or overload last night about Tremel that you took out on Karen. I know. I called Karen earlier to check if she was with you because they were going to come arrest your sorry ass again. And even though you said some things that would make you *the* prime suspect, Karen is your alibi and there's no way you did anything, regardless of what you might *wish* you had done."

"Karen wasn't with me all night..."

"Yeah, but she was with you during the news, and from what we've determined thus far Tremel was killed *before* the news. What they aired was pre-recorded. Therefore, you threatened to kill her after she was already dead. What kind of killer does that?"

"It doesn't mean I wasn't reliving past glory..."

"Shut up, Steven."

"... and your time of death could be off..."

"I said, shut up Steven!"

"Fine." Steven paused. "You know, this reminds me of that time in our senior year of high school when you and I went to Atlantic City. You didn't want to gamble too much because you were scared of what your lady would think of you if you squandered away your money like that. But after a few rounds of drinks we were really partying it up. The next morning you were freaking out because your wallet was empty, and you were certain you'd blown everything on $10 poker and cheap hookers... Of course, the fact that I told you that's where the money went helped you in that direction... but I digress. After you'd become sufficiently freaked I told you that there was no way you did what you thought. In fact, I'd taken your money the night before while you were in your drunken stupor and put it away in the hotel safe to make sure you didn't do anything remotely stupid. Remember that?"

"Actually, no I don't remember that."

"Yeah, you were pretty hammered."

"No Steven, I don't remember that because I've never been to Atlantic City. I didn't meet you until I moved here. I grew up in Detroit. I went to High School in Detroit. I've never been to Atlantic City."

"Hm. I'm pretty sure it was you."

"It wasn't me. Anyway, back to these murders; I have a suspect and we're getting a warrant to search. We're going to nail this son of a bitch, Steven, before anything else happens – and we want you to get the exclusive."

Steven's eyes were wide and eager with anticipation. "Who is it, Miles?"

"You know I can't tell you that Steven, at least not until we have the warrant."

"Miles, you know as well as I do that all I need to do is call the courthouse and they'll tell me who the warrant was issued against."

Miles scratched behind his ear and thought. "Okay, it's Jeffery Benten – the coroner's assistant."

Steven's eyes widened further. "That motherfucker's going to pay."

"Steve – we'll handle it. I'll let you know when we have more," said Miles. "In the meantime just lay low and don't do anything stupid."

Steven dropped a tip on the table and got up to leave.

"Talk to you later, Miles."[15]

---

[15]Play Audio: "Everything Starts at the Seam" by The Polyphonic Spree

Thirty-Seven

The man asleep on the couch had passed out almost before he'd finished. They'd only made it to the couch, an unfortunate truth which he'd likely chalk up as lust. She, on the other hand, had been less than impressed. She tried to be quiet on her way out, but as she was closing the door a cat tried to escape the apartment. She quickly slammed the door and was on her way.

The streets were fairly empty in this area of town. Most of the residents of the local apartments and condos were likely at work, although a few milled about in the streets, in the slow hurry of their lunch breaks. The only car she spotted was the silver Civic she'd ridden in on the way to his place. After several minutes a cab finally appeared. A wave of her hand. "Corner of Seventh and Chatham," she commanded. "Kinder-Kind."

Karen watched as Dakota pushed the cars back and forth on the play table. The other children were outside, enjoying a break in the clouds so rare in October. The cars moved slowly, gently crashing into one another, then apart, then back together. He'd been at it for a half an hour at least, and hadn't said a word, or even made eye contact, in at least twice as long.

Beverly stuck her head in through the back door leading to the playground. “Karen, someone's here to see you. She asked me through the fence if I was you and I told her you were inside. Blond lady, looks like some sort of businesswoman. I assume she doesn't know you.”

As the front door opened, Dakota's cars rolled slowly past each other, missing their crash, instead tumbling to the floor. A mop of yellow hair rounded the corner of the door and Dakota started to cry again.

Hi Alana,” said Karen. “I'm happy you were able to make it, although I couldn't imagine worse circumstances.”

“Karen?”

Karen nodded, Alana sped from the door and the two embraced. “John told me ...” Alana too started to cry. “... told me so much about you.”

“Yeah, well I'm happy to hear that. Too bad you won't be hearing any more from him.”

Alana's face was aghast. “I mean ... damn it,” Karen quickly added. “I have no idea how to deal with this. I loved him so much!”

“So did I,” replied Alana, her eyes shifting from Karen to the boy crying at the table. “Dakota. Hey there Dakota. It's your aunt Alana, remember me? You're going to come stay with me for a while.”

At that moment Beverly re-entered the room, the rest of the Kinder-Care's kids in tow. “Don't worry, I'll keep an eye on Dakota,” Beverly offered. “You know, if you two need to go talk.”

“Come on, we can talk in the break room.”

“Do you want some coffee?”

“God, I could die for some. Today's been nothing but a downer, and I really could use a pick-me-up. Nothing's been working so far.”

“So, I heard you approved an autopsy on John,” Karen blurted.

“You really do get right to the point, don't you? John always said you were honest... Yes, I approved the autopsy. But from what little I heard before I told them I didn't want to hear more, it didn't sound like there'd be much chance of an open casket anyway. Besides, anything that will help catch the fucker, pardon my French, who did this, you know?”

“Is there going to be a funeral? I assume he'll be buried next to Shawna, but I don't know how long you're planning on staying in town.”

“The service is tomorrow. It's mostly a memorial for him – a way for everyone else to say goodbye. He was, how should I put this, John was ready for death. He always had been, at least after he lost Shawna. Of course I don't think he expected it so soon, but he'd planned ahead in his own depressing, but in his mind, positive, sort of way.”

“He thought he was going to die?”

“Well not this soon, at least I don't think so. What I mean is he was prepared for death, whenever it might come. And he had a plan. You know John – any organs that can be salvaged will be donated, although I think that's going to be a total of zero. But he also had other plans of how he could still give from himself after he'd died."

"What, is he setting up some sort of trust fund or scholarship-"

"That kind of stuff is up to AHDATA," Alana interrupted. "Karen, I really don't have time to go through all of this. I just want to take Dakota and start moving forward again."

"I'm sorry," Karen replied. "You said the service is tomorrow? They're going to be done with all their tests and everything by then?"

"The service is tomorrow, but it's just a memorial. There will be a headstone placed next to Shawna's grave, but once this is all over, John's being made into a diamond."

"What?"

"A diamond, Karen – from the carbon of his body. He's being made into a diamond and the diamond will be kept safe for Dakota. If Dakota wants, John would like to be in John's fiancée's engagement ring so he can be part of Dakota's life and provide some beauty in the creation of future generations."

"Ok, first I off I had no idea they could do that."

"They can do that."

"And second off, I can't believe John never told me. That's absolutely one of the most beautiful, albeit slightly fucked-up, things I've ever heard."

"Karen, if you don't mind I'm going to take Dakota now. I'm sure I'll see you tomorrow."

"You know I'm going to be visiting," Karen fought to hold back her tears.

"Both Dakota and I would like that very much."

At that, Alana gave Karen a gentle kiss on the cheek and returned to the playroom. Karen remained seated, refusing to get up until she was certain enough time had passed for Alana and Dakota to pack up and leave. Another goodbye was beyond her.

"They're gone Karen," Beverly shouted from the adjacent room. As Karen stood she was surprised at the lack of strength in her legs. She quickly finished her coffee, reasserted herself and faced the room beyond.

"A diamond," she said to Beverly.

"What are you talking about?"

"Alana said they're going to make John into a diamond – for Dakota to give his fiancée when he grows up."

"They can do that, make someone into a diamond?"

"Yes, they can do that."

"That's one of the most fucked-up things I've ever heard."

"I don't know... I think it's kind of beautiful. Shine on, John."

Thirty-Eight

"Where the hell have you been? I've been trying to reach you all day. I was just about to give the Tremel story to Simkin."

"The Tremel story?"

"You did hear what happened, didn't you? I talked to your buddy Miles and he said he told you all about it."

"Is this Fred?"

"Damn right it's Fred. I left you at least a dozen messages today. You need to check your phone more often."

"Oh, you mean the story about how that dumb bitch got her head cut off." The red light on Steven's answering machine was blinking. He pressed the button marked *Erase All*. "In retrospect, the whole head seems like overkill. Maybe just the nose would have been better, since she was always sticking it too far in to where it didn't belong. Plus eyes are *so yesterday*, and a nose would have been much cheaper for postage. Then again, the head wasn't actually *mailed*, so I guess that doesn't matter.

“What the hell is wrong with you? Are you writing the story or not? I need it by the end of the night.”

“Yeah, I've got the story. Should be easy.” Steven paused. “What else did Miles tell you?”

“He said you were acting stranger than usual. I didn't believe him ... I do now.”

“Whatever Fred. Talk to you later.”

“Steven,” Fred's voice took a serious tone. “You're not my friend, but if you were, I'd recommend you straighten your shit out and try not to piss anyone off. They aren't liking you too much downtown right now, and I've heard there are some people at the precinct who are eager to get you back down there. You might want to do your research via phone this time.”

“Fred, stop worrying. You're story will be perfect. I have an inside source.”

“Hm. Miles didn't seem to know too much about this one from what he told me earlier.”

“Not Miles, Fred.” Steven hung up the phone, picked it back up and dialed.

Thirty-Nine

"I told you, I'm not coming over tonight."

"Don't tell me you couldn't use some relaxation."

"Dammit Steven, today was bad enough. I don't need you making it any worse."

"What do you mean, making it worse?" Steven asked, his tone incredulous.

"You honestly don't get it, do you? I. Want. To. Be. Alone. I don't even want to talk right now."

"Sex then? I promise I'll keep my mouth shut."

"Fuck you, Steven."

"Ok, now we're getting somewhere."

"Don't you even care how things went with Dakota today? You don't give a shit about me, do you? That's a rhetorical question. Of course you don't give a shit about me. You used to, or maybe I gave a shit about you once, but ... ugh, you're such an asshole."

"I'm sorry," Steven sighed. "How did things go with Dakota today?"

"I don't even know. It was horrible. It was fine. I guess it went the only way it could go, which is the way it went. I don't even know if Dakota has any idea what's going on. He's a smart kid, so maybe he does, but maybe that's even worse. Either way, he's gone now and John's going to be a diamond."

"A diamond?"

"Alana's having him cremated and turned into a diamond or something." Karen was exasperated. "I don't want to go through explaining it. Look it up on the Internet."

"You know, you get pissed off at me because you think I don't care. Then I ask a question, like I *do care* and you get even more pissed off. What am I supposed to do? You act like everything in this relationship is 100% you, but you don't give a flying fuck how *I* feel. You don't know the first thing about me. You don't know what I dream about, you don't know what I do when you're not around, and you sure as hell don't seem to care about finding out."

"Relationship? This isn't a relationship Steven, it's a one-way street to hell and I keep getting run over while I travel it. How's that for a relationship?"

"Are we done? I have a story to write."

"Oh, we're done Steven."

Karen slammed the phone back into its cradle, and not knowing whether she should scream or cry, went to her desk and got out her diary. She opened it up and paged through the faded contents. She thumbed past the pages chronicling her high school crushes, and came across a blank page.[16]

It's been a long time since I wrote in here. Way too long, really. Over the years I've read and re-read my dreams and hopes from my youth, but haven't gotten the courage to revisit these pages with a pen.

My life is a mess. This is nothing like my dreams. This is nothing like the fairytale I dreamt about long ago. It was for a while, especially with John, even though he wasn't mine. Just having him near me was enough. But life shouldn't be lived vicariously, and this sudden realization of my actual life is heartbreaking, to say the least.

I can't honestly recall what it was that I loved about Steven, or if I loved him at all. Perhaps my life has been nothing more than holding on to a dream and wishing it true, the flash of magic from the wish blinding me from reality.

Today when Alana came to pick up Dakota, it was as if John were back, even though it wasn't him. Her grey-blue eyes held that same sparkle I always loved in John's. I know Dakota will be fine. He'll be loved.

I need to be loved. Or maybe I just want to be loved.

First, I need to love myself.

Steven... I don't know what to do with Steven.

---

[16]Play Audio: "One By One" by Billy Bragg and Wilco

Maybe more time needs to pass before I can see things clearly again. Then again, maybe now I'm seeing things clearly for the first time in a long time.

Time is needed.

John, if you're over my shoulder reading this, "Shine on, you crazy diamond."

William F. Aicher

Day Five

PENANCE[17]

[17]Play Audio: “Don't Get Lost In Heaven” by Gorillaz

William F. Aicher

Forty

Steven's eyes opened suddenly. He'd had the dream again, but this time he had been paying attention.

He peeled the damp, sweaty sheets away from his body, moved to his writing desk, brought the computer back up from hibernation and double-clicked the file labeled simply, "For Fred." The document opened, he scrolled to the place where he'd left off earlier, and he began to type.

After some time had passed, Steven clicked the save button and then the print button. The ancient inkjet on the desk slowly spit out the pages, minute by minute. He slid his story into a crisp manila envelope, closed the clasp and returned to his bed.

Babies would have been jealous of the sleep he enjoyed for the night's remainder.

Forty-One

The sunlight streaming in through the window crept across the desk, bathing the pages of her diary with the glow of morning. Dust motes flitted about, pushed away by Karen's sleeping breath, never quite landing on the illuminated pages. As the sun casually rose, a beam caught on the silver of Karen's pen, the sharp glint waking her.

She embraced the sun's warmth as she too rose, fully appreciating the return of light. The timer on her coffee maker sounded, and the beans she'd put in the night before met their end as the grinder whirred to life. The smell of new day filled her nostrils.

After pouring herself a cup of coffee, she returned to her bedroom and closed the diary she'd written in the night before, placing it back on the shelf where it belonged. This was the most refreshed and *whole* she'd felt in ages. Shedding herself of yesterday's clothes, she made her way to the bathroom and enjoyed an unnecessarily long shower.

Just as she finished putting on her robe, the phone rang. It was Miles.

"Karen, have you heard from Steven?"

"Not since last night, why?"

Forty-Two[18]

Three hours earlier, Miles had been sound asleep at home, snuggled up next to his wife Thalia. He was woken from his dreams by the buzzing of his phone as it vibrated on his nightstand. He answered the call and exited the warmth of the bed.

"I have to go in, honey," he said, and kissed his wife on the forehead.

"Is everything okay?" Thalia groaned. She rolled over and Miles kissed her again, on the back of her neck.

"Don't worry. I'll be home soon. Tell the boys I love them."

Miles dressed and got into his car and drove back into downtown Courtsdale. The streets were empty at this late hour, and so after a short twenty minute drive he arrived at his destination.

Fallimore Park lay in the heart of Courtsdale, just off the main city plaza. The location had previously been home to the original grounds of the Courtsdale Community College, before it relocated to a larger campus on the west side of town. Most of the building had since been razed,

---

[18]Play Audio: "King of All the World" by The Old 97's

except for the old band shelter, which had been renovated and transformed into a public performance shelter when the land was converted into a city park.

Due to its location in the heart of downtown, the park was one of the most popular relaxation destinations for both citizens and visitors alike. A small pond situated on the park's South side offered relaxation, with a selection of rowboats available for public use. The park's variety of trails invited walkers, bikers and rollerskaters. Young couples enjoyed picnics daily in the grassy places, protected in the shade of trees, while the older generations challenged each other to games of chess and checkers.

Miles walked across the park, toward the pond. The pond's shore was one of the more popular gathering areas for the chess and checker aficionados. A circle of policemen were gathered around one of the tables. Lieutenant Pickerson looked up from the group, and motioned for Miles to come to him.

What Miles saw made him sick. There, on the concrete gaming table, lay a dead body, stripped completely naked. The table supported the victim's back and lower abdomen, leaving the legs to hang down. The neck had also been cut, allowing the head to dangle freely, making the man's chest the focal point of the display.

The victim, black man, had a series of alternating squares cut into his chest and abdomen. Plastic checker pieces were placed among the black squares, the squares of the man's skin. Deep inside a cluster of black pieces where one player would have sat, lay a lone red checker, a scrap of paper sticking out from underneath. Miles reached for it.

“Don't touch that, detective. We're still cataloging the scene.”

Miles felt his mind snap back to reality. He looked at his Lieutenant, then back down at the body in front of him. He bent down to his knees and looked at the victim's upside down face. It was Jeffrey Benten.

"Looks to me like he's not our guy, hey Detective?"

"It doesn't rule him out, Lieutenant."

"Maybe not, but I think this might." Pickerson pointed to the piece of paper on the man's chest. "It's a note."

"What does it-"

"Two hand-written words: 'King Me.' Do you have any idea what that means?"

"No sir, I'm afraid I don't."

"It means you were wrong, Detective." Pickerson was agitated. "It also means that whoever did this very likely was aware of the details of our investigation and wanted to make it absolutely clear that we had the wrong suspect. Either that, or it's a very unlikely circumstance, and in my thirty-five years of experience I don't believe in chance."

"May I see the note, sir?" asked Miles, reaching for the scrap of paper.

"*Hands off, Detective!* As I said, we're still cataloging. You can look at it here."

Pickerson reached into his pocket, took out a small silver digital camera and turned it on. Miles took the camera and looked at the LCD screen. He flipped through the pictures on the memory card until he arrived at the photos of the paper. He stopped and zoomed in on the first one.

"Oh shit," he muttered. "Can you excuse me, Lieutenant? I need to make a phone call."

Forty-Three

"Karen, have you heard from Steven?"

"Not since last night, why?" The phone was slippery in her sweaty grip.

"You're back from his place already?"

"Actually, I spent the night here last night. I didn't even go to Steven's. We had a bit of an argument."

"What about?"

"I was having a good morning Miles. Can we please not talk about Steven?"

"... I'm worried about him, Karen."

"I'm not."

"Come on Karen, seriously. He seemed ... odd ... the last time I talked to him. You didn't notice anything?"

"Other than the fact that he was a complete asshole again?"

“Well, let me know if you hear from him, ok?” Miles sounded frantic. “I *really* need to talk to him.”

Karen sighed. “Fine. I'm going to go now Miles. I'll talk to you later.”

No sooner had she hung up than it began to ring again.

“What now, Miles?”

“Karen, it's Fred – Steven's boss.”

Karen paused. She'd never spoken with Fred before, let alone chatted on the telephone. “Oh, hi Fred... is there something I can help you with?”

“Have you heard from Steven?”

“That seems to be the question of the day today,” Karen replied. “No, I haven't heard from him. Why, is something the matter?”

“He was supposed to get me a story on the Tremel murder last night – a follow-up to the reporting he's been doing on this recent spree going on. Anyway, he never dropped it off. I checked my e-mail, just in case he'd decided to embrace technology finally, but nothing there either.”

“Steven and I ... if I talk to Steven, I'll let him know you called and to get you the story ASAP.”

“Don't worry about the story. I had Simkin come in late last night to finish up the draft he'd started when I couldn't get hold of Steven in the first place. If you talk to Steven, just make sure he calls me. I've just about had it with him lately.”

“Will do. Bye Fred.”

Karen hung up the phone and called Miles back.

"Miles, it's Karen. I just got a call from Steven's boss."

"Steven's *boss* called you?"

"That's what I said. Anyway," *How does Steven wreck my day without even being in it*? "I'm starting to get worried about Steven, but I really don't want to talk to him. Can you give him a call and check in on him?"

"I already tried him – must have called at least a half dozen times. I just keep getting his machine."

Dread washed over Karen. *Oh God, not Steven too.*

"Miles, can you go over there? I need to know he's ok."

"I'm downtown right now, but I'm already on my way to the car. I should be to his place within the hour."

"Thank you so much." *Please don't be too late.*

Forty-Four

Miles pressed the buzzer for Apartment 4F a third time. "Steven, I said it's Miles. If you don't answer you know I'll just come in anyway – probable cause, and all that."

The security door clicked and unlocked.

"Come on up."

With the shades closed and the apartment lights off, it was difficult for Miles to make out Steven's face. But somewhere under the frazzled mop of hair, unshaven face and dirty bathrobe before him hid his pal.

"Sorry the place is such a mess. I've been busy on a story I'm writing for *The Courier* and really haven't had time for much else."

As his eyes adjusted to the light, Miles looked around the room and realized it in fact was a mess – much more of a mess than Steven's usual mess. The clothes Steven had been wearing when they'd met the day before were strewn about the apartment floor, as if Steven had taken them off right there when he got home the previous night. Banky's litter box sat in the corner, a pile of wet turds sat next to it.

"Your house is disgusting, Steven – but it looks better than you do right now."

"How I look is of little matter, Miles. Like I said, *I've been writing.* Fred wanted a story, and I have written my best story yet. I'd say it's the greatest story ever told, but that's already reserved for the bible ... the bible is a great story, isn't it?"

"Yeah, I guess. I haven't read it in a while."

"You really must read it again. It's full of so many *dastardly* things. There's rape and incest and torture and killing – and it's all in the name of God. I was thinking about it the other day, you know, after Father Bergens was killed, and it occurred to me just how *fucked up* it is that people actually go out of their way to *worship* someone as utterly horrifying as god."

"Yeah, whatever Steve. Where were you last night?"

"It's Steven."

"*Steven.* I came over here to check on you for Karen. I promised her I'd make sure you were okay, and you seem to be. Whether or not you'll be alive later after everything you must have drunk last night is another issue, but it's not one I feel like dealing with."

"Oh, I didn't drink at all last night. I told you, I was writing. Did I mention I had more dreams too? Dreams and writing. I think that's how it went at least. I'm fairly positive I didn't *dream* that I was writing."

Steven quickly turned, ran across the room and jumped over the couch. He reached down to the coffee table and picked up a crisp manila envelope.

"Can you do me a favor on your way downtown today? Can you please drop this off at *The Courier* for me? I'd say 'pretty please,' but I have a sneaking suspicion I don't look very pretty right now."

Miles reached for the envelope in Steven's hands and stopped, eyeing it curiously. "What is it?"

"I *told you Miles*. I wrote a story."

"You were here last night, writing this?"

Steven nodded.

"All night?"

"Where else would I have been? Karen didn't want to talk to me and you were already home for the night."

Miles took the envelope. "I'm pretty sure they don't need this anymore. Karen said Fred called and said Simkin wrote the story for you."

Steven was starting to lose his patience. "Just drop it off for me anyway. It's way better than the story Fred originally asked for. What I've got in there is going to blow this whole murder thing wide open."

"Steven, I just..." Miles paused. "... if there are things in here that you know that you aren't sharing with the police, it could be very bad."

"You and your cop friends will find out about it soon enough. Journalistic privilege, my dear Miles."

Miles hesitated, took the envelope and turned for the door.

“We're friends Miles. No peeking.”

Forty-Five

Fred fingered the manila envelope on his desk lightly. *Too flat for a head ... maybe a tongue? Or some skin? I really shouldn't open this.*

FOR YOUR EYES ONLY

ATTN: FRED, THE BOSS-MAN
COURTSDALE COURIER

2727 WEST MAIN STREET

COURTSDALE

"Where'd this package come from?' Fred asked out loud to the room.

"A detective dropped it off for you while you were at lunch, sir,' answered Sara Dawkins, his secretary. "He said Steven Carvelle asked him to bring it by. He said Steven said you'd be expecting it."

A little late, Carvelle. "Did he say anything else? Like where Carvelle *is,* or why this story is *ten hours past deadline*?"

“No sir, he just dropped it off.”

'Hmph.” He bent back the clasps on the envelope, pulled out the document within, and began reading.

The Trouble with Being God

By Steven Carvelle

The Courtsdale Carver. This could be his name. The fact that he has no name, at least not one that we've been made aware of, makes it ever so difficult to speak of him – or her, for that matter. Then again, this is a serial killer who is stalking the streets of Courtsdale, and nearly every serial killer in the history of time has been a male. Therefore, from here on, I will be referring to “him” as him. As for the name “The Courtsdale Carver,” well that's simply so we can be civilized. One cannot speak in pronouns alone, for fear of becoming too personally attached.

Once again, the carver has struck out against the powerful in this town. The latest in his rash of gruesome murders was none other than one Mary Tremel, of the Channel Four news team. This murder follows in the footsteps of the death and mutilations, previously reported by yours truly, of both Father Theodore Bergens and Mr. John Paluniak, former head of AHDATA.

What one generally looks for in cases of these types are ways in which they are tied together. A motive. A mode of operation. No doubt this is where Courtsdale's finest officers are currently focusing their efforts (although rumor has it that help from the FBI's Behavioral Science Unit is on its way. Whether this was by request, or by force, is up to speculation).

But isn't the driving force behind this all perfectly clear? Those who have been killed are people who all once enjoyed some amount of power. They were all gods of their own domains, and they commanded the respect of others. In fact, their command for respect actually went so far as to actually have followers. People gathered to worship every week with Father Bergens, Mr. Paluniak's AHDATA was nearing an almost cult-like status, and Ms. Tremel's fan club was nearly idolatry.

The person who is behind this is very likely one who feels threatened by these types of worship. The person behind all of this is God. Or at least someone who believes they are God (or at least working on His behalf). And this person is striking back in the way the religious and righteous have always done so, by smiting those who stand in the way.

Father Bergens was crucified. John Paluniak was forced to look to the heavens. And Mary Tremel, well she was beheaded just like John the Baptist – and her head was delivered on a silver plate.

"Populus vulti decipi, decipiatur."

"The people want to be deceived. Let them be deceived." It's a quote Carlo Cardinal Caraffa said once about religion. It's also the quote that was delivered with Tremel's head.

Of course, this may all sound like pure speculation. And of course it would be, if we didn't have some sort of facts, some sort of source.

This story is written to reveal that source, a revelation which will lead to the end of the Courtsdale Carver.

Forty-Six

"Miles, it's Karen. I just heard from Steven."

"Oh crap. I'm sorry Karen; I completely forgot to call you after I went over there."

"It's fine Miles. Steven just returned my call; he says he's fine. I'm actually on my way over there now. He said he wants to talk."

Miles hesitated. "Are you sure he's fine, Karen? When I was over there earlier he seemed to be far from fine. In fact, I would say he was the opposite of fine. He looked a mess, and he was acting strange - stranger than usual, I mean. Besides, I saw something earlier that-"

"I'm sure it's fine Miles. He was probably just upset about last night. I think it will be good for both of us if we talk about things for once, and it sounds like he's ready to do that now."

"Okay Karen, I trust you, but I need you to promise to call me if you need me or if anything seems strange or uncomfortable when you're over there with Steven. Anything at all."

Forty-Seven

The Courtsdale Carver BELIEVES he is GOD. Or at least he believed it at one time. He was sick and tired of people worshipping others besides him. It had gone on for too long AND HE SMOTE THEM DOWN WITH HIS WRATH.

And I will continue to smite them! There is still one more who has done wrong. One more who has denied me. She's denied me time and time again, at night, when I'm dreaming, before the cock crows. Cutting, tasting, and beating her fucking skull in. On the concrete before me, she will worship.

With all the dreams I've been having, there is one thing I can take comfort in. And that is the fact that they are my dreams. If they weren't my dreams, if they weren't something I decided, subconsciously even, that is when I would start to be truly worried.

I now know what I need to do to make the dream go away.

I believed I was perfect – that I was a god, but the things I do are better than anything god ever did, because they are real.

The trouble with being god is that god's not real.

I am real. Love me.

"Sara, get me the police. Now."

Forty-Eight

The basement storage unit at Steven's apartment was deserted. The floor itself consisted of nothing but bare poured concrete. The corridor leading between the chicken-wire protected storage units was lit by a row of light bulbs spaced just far enough apart that the light from one didn't quite overlap the light from the next.

Steven stood in the middle of his unit and looked at the stacks of cardboard boxes filled with old sweaters and even older memories that surrounded him. The boxes on the floor were damp and smelled of mildew, victims of the seepage problem that plagued the basement during heavy rains. He pulled an old wooden chair from a corner, wiped the accumulated dust with the sleeve of his sweatshirt and sat, placing his duffel bag on the floor in front of him.

He reached down, unzipped the bag, reached inside and retrieved the only item within – a shiny new straight-blade razor, stolen from a local barbershop earlier that day. Holding the blade in his hand, he gazed at the reflection staring back. He showed no surprise when in the reflection, from one of the darkened corners of the room, a man stepped forward.

"I was wondering when you'd show up," Steven said.

The man stepped forward and Steven turned in his chair, remaining seated. He appeared to be a stranger, although the shadows that fell across his face made it impossible to say for certain.

"Have you?" asked the intruder.

"Of course I have. I finally figured it out last night."

"What, exactly, did you figure out?" asked the man, inquisitively.

"I figured out what I have to do. Or, maybe I should say, what *we* have to do."

"We?" asked the man.

The man's face remained shrouded in darkness. Unable to make out his face, Steven noticed the man was about the same height as Steven – the same build. He was dressed simply: a pair of torn jeans, a black t-shirt and a pair of black sneakers.

"We, me, whatever is the right way to say it," Steven replied. "During my dream last night I realized that it really has been me all along. I didn't remember any of what I'd done, because everything I did happened after I'd been drinking. That's when you come out – after I've been drinking. Now you're here though, and I haven't been drinking. You're here because I've come to accept that you're inside me and I've decided to finally let you out."

"I see…" said the man in the corner.

"So after we do this, which one of us is the one who remains? Or will the Jekyll and Hyde continue?"

"You really have no idea what you're talking about, do you?"

"Of course I do," Steven replied. "I have to kill Karen. That's what happens next."

Forty-Nine

"Steven, are you there?" Karen pressed the buzzer for 4F a third time. After receiving no response, she walked back to the main gate, and noticed a small post-it note stuck to it.

Karen, getting some things from storage. Meet me in the basement.

To allow for easier move-ins, the apartment's basement storage area was accessible from the parking lot as well as from the main building. To get in to the main building from the storage area still required a key, but access to the storage area was open. Karen walked through the lot and went down the stairs.

A security camera was mounted at the bottom of the staircase, where the corridor began. Karen doubted it actually worked.

"Steven, are you down here?"

Fifty

Miles sped across town, dialing Karen's cell phone time after time, only to get her voicemail. He'd tried calling Steven as well, but again only got the machine. The call he'd received from *The Courier* had been frantic, but it had reinforced his new, although heartbreaking, theory: Steven Carvelle was the Courtsdale Carver.

While the rest of the police squad was busy assembling, Miles had decided to act on his own. Karen was on her way to Steven's, and from what he'd heard, it sure as hell sounded like Steven planned to kill her.

After arriving at the apartment complex, Miles nearly jumped out of the car before stopping. He ran to the security gate at the front of the building, pressing the buzzer for Steven's apartment, just in case. After no response, he pulled out his gun, aimed it at the lock on the security door, and was stopped by the sound of a piercing scream from the parking lot. He pulled his gun to a defensive firing position, and took off in the direction of the scream.

Another scream. This time Miles was certain it was Karen.

“Karen, this is detective Miles. Are you hurt?”

“Miles!” Karen screamed his name. “I need you Miles!”

Fifty-One

"I have to kill Karen. That's what happens next."

"You see, this is why *I* have to do what I'm about to. At first you were a nuisance, but things have escalated. I know about your article, and I am not about to let some uninspiring writer and pathetic drunk try to take claim for what I've done."

Steven stood up and faced the man directly. Only then did he see the hatchet in the stranger's hand.

"Where'd that come from?" Steven asked." I didn't bring it. I don't even own a hatchet." He suddenly felt very sick, and his heart began to race.

"I'd normally take my time and enjoy myself, but you weren't part of the plan." With his other hand, the stranger reached into his pants pocket and pulled out a small rosary.

"You, Steven Carvelle, have become a problem," said the Stranger. "Here - you're going to need this where you're going." He tossed the rosary to Steven, who reached up to catch it. In the distraction he didn't see the man advance, hatchet raised high.

Steven opened his mouth to scream, but was silenced as the blade caught his lower jaw, severing it instantly. To his right he heard foot-steps. In shock, he turned to face their direction, saw Karen stop at the door and heard her let out a blood-curdling scream.

The stranger hauled back the hatchet and landed a second blow, this time directly to Steven's chest. There it remained, lodged in his ribcage, as the stranger ran toward the door, shoving Karen aside as he exited.

Karen rushed to Steven's side, took him in her arms and screamed again. She felt Steven's body spasm in her embrance. "Miles!" she screamed. "I need you Miles!" she sobbed.

Miles ran down the corridor, gun still at the ready, and turned the corner into the open storage unit. Karen knelt before him on the floor, next to Steven.

Unable to speak, Steven reached up to the bloody mass where his mouth had been and took a handful of blood. He reached out to one of the still un-stained areas of concrete, and with his red hands, wrote "I was wrong. Forgive me."

Karen turned to face Miles, tears streaming down her cheeks.

"Karen, who did this?" Miles asked.

Unable to speak, Karen pointed toward the door and the trail of bloody shoeprints the stranger had left behind.

Miles ran off in pursuit and Steven's body fell limp.[19]

[19] Play Audio: "Feel to Believe" by Beth Orton

CPSIA information can be obtained at www.ICGtesting.com
Printed in the USA
BVOW08s2152300616
454170BV00001B/24/P